"Don't make a sound," *the outlaw whispered, reaching under her dress. "Not a word...."*

In the haze of a dream—the aftermath of the fantasy she'd had before drifting off to sleep, one that seemed incredibly real—Nicki felt the outlaw's hands on her rear end, cupping her.

Don't make a sound. And she didn't as her face rubbed against her bedcovers, her hands pressed against the mattress. Her breasts were flattened beneath her, making them feel swollen, raw against the quilting.

In that foggy dream, she felt the bed dip as the bandit climbed onto it, heard the box springs creak. His legs brushed the outside of hers as he straddled her.

"You're probably wondering why I'm here," he said in a deep Western drawl, a whisper above the stillness of the night. He slipped his hands—big, work-roughened hands—from her butt to her hips, then...

"You knew this is the only place I can hide out. You waited for me," he said, stroking her softness until she was ready to scream.

Yes. And he was definitely worth the wait....

DQ670961

Dear Reader,

I've always *loved* a fun sexual romp story. So when my editor suggested that I write a role-playing book, I seized the opportunity to couple a romp with other favorites: outlaw, pirate and harem tales and, of course, the vampire "victim" fantasy.

So come on in and meet Nicki Wade, who's spent so much effort working to get her ranch back on its feet that she hasn't had much time for romance. But when her hot next-door neighbor comes back to town, she ends up in bed with him...and he ends up being a very real part in *her* fantasies!

Surely you could use a little play in your life, too.... ;)

It'd be wonderful if you could check out my romance site at www.crystal-green.com, where I run contests and keep you up to date on my releases!

Happy reading,

Crystal Green

Crystal Green

ROPED IN

TORONTO NEW YORK LONDON
AMSTERDAM PARIS SYDNEY HAMBURG
STOCKHOLM ATHENS TOKYO MILAN MADRID
PRAGUE WARSAW BUDAPEST AUCKLAND

Recycling programs
for this product may
not exist in your area.

ISBN-13: 978-0-373-79653-3

ROPED IN

For questions and comments about the quality of this book
please contact us at Customer_eCare@Harlequin.ca.

www.Harlequin.com

Printed in U.S.A.

ABOUT THE AUTHOR

Crystal Green lives near Las Vegas, where she writes for the Harlequin Special Edition and Blaze lines. She loves to read, overanalyze movies and TV programs, practice yoga and travel when she can. You can read more about her at www.crystal-green.com, where she has a blog and contests. Also, you can follow her on Facebook at www.facebook.com/people/Chris-Marie-Green/1051327765 and Twitter at www.twitter.com/ChrisMarieGreen.

Books by Crystal Green

To Lisa Kessler and Melissa Cutler for the title suggestion, as well as all the wonderful authors in RWA-SD who came up with title ideas! You guys are the best organization a gal could hope for.

SHE WAS A REAL VISION tonight, wearing a purple corset, a boa and a ruffled satin skirt that lifted in the front to show off fishnet-stocking legs and ankle-high boots.

A saloon girl who was made to draw every gaze in the room.

And every time Nicki Wade caught a glimpse of her Halloween-party self in one of the mirrors of the Pine Junction Grand Hotel ballroom, she kept thinking, *Who knew?*

"Told you," said her cousin Candace as they waited for the band to start up again. "Can I cook, or can I cook?"

Nicki cut her gaze from the mirror, smiling at Candace. Dress up. It reminded her of all those days when her cousin would stay on the ranch during the summer, giving her single, divorced mom a break. Like sisters, the same age with the same youthful energies, they'd spent rainy days in the attic, wearing old clothes, acting like princesses and belles, even though Nicki had been far from either.

"I can't complain about a makeover," she said.

Candace tugged on one of Nicki's curls. "I did have some good raw material to work with. You were made for more than jeans and boots, Nic."

Not for the first time, Nicki touched the silk of her costume. Shiny as a rainy-day fantasy. Decadent as one of the heroines in the novels that had always drawn her to the corner of the second-hand bookshop in town—the ones shelved under the label Lusty Historical, where the women wore corsets and garters as a matter of everyday necessity.

Candace linked arms with her. *She* was dressed as a sexy cowgirl, all in white, from the hat that covered her long red hair to the bikini top and chaps that revealed a body honed by her time jogging on the beach near the apartment she'd recently needed to vacate. As always, though, Pine Junction hadn't been too far for her. It was about an hour from the San Diego shoreline, but a world away in attitude, tucked into the trees of the eastern part of the county, which was dotted with ranches.

"So," Candace said, "now that I've gotten you out of the Square W+W ranch office, it's time to have some fun. Do you see anything here that you like?"

Slipping her arm out of Candace's, Nicki leaned back against a tall, linen-draped table littered with empty bottles and surveyed the room, but just as usual, the men didn't much catch her fancy.

There had always been only one guy who'd ever done that, and he'd left town a long time ago. He'd be a man now, not a boy, and not the seventeen-year-old who'd left after an infamous tear-down fight with his dad.

Candace laughed. "I know who you're looking for."

No use hiding it from her only cousin. Candace had

grown up knowing all about Nicki, thanks to the letters they wrote when they weren't together and the secrets they'd shared when they were.

"You don't have to say it," Nicki said, fighting the heat on her skin. "Shane Carter's back, and I can't keep my eyes from the doorway."

"And he's been here for two days already. All you had to do was go next door, bring him some welcome-home cookies—"

"It's not that easy."

"Sure it is."

Nicki shook her head. Candace knew how Nicki had spun a million fantasies about Shane. He'd been a couple years older, one of those boys at school whom everyone kept their eye on. Whatever he tried—baseball, football—he was good at, although he never showed much interest in pursuing any of them. No, standoffish Shane was far better at getting into mischief on and off the ranch.

But that didn't mean there wasn't a heart beneath his bad-boy exterior. She'd seen it once, way back when she'd been about nine and had been playing around with Candace, using the fence that separated their properties as a balance beam.

Just as they'd seen Mr. Carter and Shane riding up in the distance, that rail had split beneath Nicki, and she'd tumbled to the ground.

She'd heard Mr. Carter yelling at her about ruining his property, just before Shane had jumped off his horse, making sure she was all right, then covering her as his father had approached.

Both she and Candace had seen it—a standoff between a wiry, protective eleven-year-old kid and his livid father, who was said to have a terrible temper. And she'd never forgotten how a red-faced Mr. Carter had ridden off after giving Shane a look that said punishment would be in store for him back at the house.

Without commenting on it, Shane made double sure that Nicki was okay, then rode off, too, the sunlight burnishing him as he took her heart with him.

That was really when he'd become the prince in every fairy tale for Nicki. Then, after she'd graduated to more adult books, she'd pictured him as every hero, even as he'd become Pine Junction's Romeo in reality, going from playing pranks in town to rankling just about every father in the area with his love-'em-and-leave-'em ways.

Funny thing was that Nicki had never stopped putting him on a romantic pedestal. She'd measured every man against him and they'd all come up short to the fantasy.

She stopped looking around the room at the other guys. "I don't know why Shane's home or how long he'll be there, so why bother him?"

"Because—"

"Candy, Shane can't be back in town for any good reason." His dad had died a few years ago and his older brother, Tommy, had deserted the Slanted C Ranch out of the blue. Shane hadn't even visited over the years.

"Don't you wonder," Candace said, "what he might be like now? Isn't that driving you crazy?"

Nicki's belly flipped from a mixture of anticipation and fear of disappointment.

"I've wondered," she finally said. "But that still doesn't mean I'm going over there with cookie plate in hand."

"But this is finally your chance."

Nicki just smiled. She'd had plenty of dreams about what she'd do with Shane if she had any kind of chance.

"See?" Candace said, nudging her. "All you need is a push forward. Come on, admit it—if you had an opportunity with Shane, you'd…"

Nicki's smile grew even bigger as she took a drink of beer, and Candace laughed again.

"Told you," she said.

There wasn't much use in talking about Shane, so Nicki rested her icy bottle against her neck, wallowing in the glass's coolness. The ballroom's ceiling fans were trying like the dickens to chase away the Indian summer, but they were hardly doing a good job of it.

Looking at all the other sexy costumes around the room, she thought that if Shane *were* to amble in here, he wouldn't get past the door, where there was a shapely fairy lingering with a very un-Disney-ish princess whose Fantasylands were having a hard time staying in their bodices.

She officially changed the subject. "And here I thought the Halloween season is supposed to be scary. Isn't it about ghouls and goblins rather than little French maid costumes?"

Candace sighed, obviously wanting to get back to the Shane conversation. "Halloween time is *always* a good time to show off what God gave a girl." She held her champagne as if she was at some kind of rooftop shindig in downtown San Diego instead of tiny Pine Junction. "It's a time when we can put the *va* in our *voom* and get away with it."

Near the dance floor, Nicki couldn't help but notice that a few hands from neighboring ranches were hanging out, eyeing Candace. And, if she didn't know better, she'd say that they were taking her in, too, as if they'd just now noticed that she existed beyond the confines of the Square W+W Ranch.

And why not? She'd just about been a self-imposed prisoner there, working away in the office, burying herself in the account books and hardly ever going out until Candace had settled into the house on the ranch a week ago.

"See?" Candace said, noticing the cowpokes, too. "You've already been staked out, and those guys just walked into the room."

Nicki's skin flushed. Thing was, now that she'd been thinking of Shane, she'd lost all interest. Maybe it was a sign of laziness that she buried herself in the safety of her fantasies. Maybe she just didn't have the energy, what with all the work waiting for her back in real life.

Still, she gave the guys a subtle yet thorough scan. She didn't know these particular cowpokes—maybe they were new hires at one of the ranches in the area— but then again, she hadn't socialized so much recently. Come to think of it, even before her parents had been killed in an auto accident out on the infamous Drop Curve on the highway a few years ago and left her with a failing ranch, she hadn't been all that sociable. Her family had always lived hand-to-mouth, and to combat that, she'd grown up focused, devoting herself to the support of their always-wavering American Paint horse breeding operation. At the end of the day, she'd recline on the porch and read rummage-sale books until someone called her in for dinner.

Maybe she'd never given life a chance outside of her comfort zone, but, realistically, Nicki was pretty sure that one makeover wasn't going to change everything in a single night. She wouldn't suddenly not be a bookworm who'd had about one significant relationship in her life. And that man, Arthur, had dropped her without all that much fanfare after she'd *really* gotten in deep with her work at the ranch.

Even now, as she thought of the W+W, she got a little unsociable again.

What was she doing? She didn't have time for silly games with men like these, anyway, not when tomorrow was a big day for the ranch.

The big day.

Candace said, "Would you just relax?"

"Can't. Tomorrow keeps eating away at me."

"You're going to do fine. *We'll* do fine. That ranch is a second home to me, and I'm not about to see it go under." She drank her champagne. "It'll be bad enough seeing it go dude."

"I know."

They'd heard through the grapevine that a corporate investment firm had been nosing around some property in these parts, asking about possibilities for a dude resort. Nicki had spent some sleepless nights working things out in her head. She'd already sold off most of the horse stock after her parents' deaths, and she'd been doing everything possible to keep from laying off any of the employees, who were just like family.

Going dude seemed like the only option, as long as the investors agreed to keep the staff on. And at least it would maintain the ranch, which went back generations in her family.

So she'd contacted the Lyon Group and invited one

of their representatives to the Square W+W so he could see how perfect it would be for the company's purposes.

Candace was watching a mobile of flying ghoulies that dangled from the ceiling. "I shouldn't get on your case about nerves. What you're doing is important. There're other families who've been working on the ranch for years, too, and they could lose a home just as much as you could, if you don't turn everything around."

"Thanks for understanding," Nicki said.

"You know I'd do anything for you." Candace slowly put down her nearly empty champagne flute. "And I'd do anything for your mom and dad, too."

Candace's voice was thick, and Nicki rested a hand over hers.

She didn't say anything more, not until Candace put on a happier face, which Nicki knew was meant for her sake.

"To life," Candace said, raising what was left of her champagne. "To things getting better from this point on."

They toasted, as if it didn't matter that life had spiraled downward for all of them recently. Candace herself had been going through hard times, laid off as a personal assistant at an electronics firm, where she'd been involved with a corporate internship program and riding her ambition toward a bright future...until the newest employees had fallen under the ax. Now, with her pocketbook nearly empty from the same hard times that were affecting everyone, she was staying with Nicki for a few months so she could save up enough money to go back out on her own again.

Out of the corner of her eye, Nicki saw one of the ranch hands glancing her way again.

As if looking for something positive to latch on to after the heavy moment, Candace said, "Ah. The saloon girl costume. It does it for a guy every single time."

"How would you know?"

"Halloween isn't the only time a girl can dress up."

Candace just kept smiling, and Nicki got the feeling they weren't talking about the upcoming holiday itself anymore.

"Candy...?"

Seeming mighty innocent, Candace ran a finger around the rim of her champagne glass, then smirked.

Nicki recognized the gesture from times gone by, such as the day Candace had instigated a "stakeout" in the old barn, where they knew Johnny Graystone and Jane Willens met every day to smooch. They'd giggled all through the make-out session until Johnny had discovered them and chased them out.

"I'm just telling you," Candace said. "If you want, you could get a lot of mileage out of this costume. And don't tell me it hasn't crossed your mind, Miss Romance. There are guys out there who'd like a little taste of this in real life...or at least as real as fantasies can get."

"Are you talking about...?"

"Taking the saloon girl out of the party and to the bedroom? You know I am."

Nicki wasn't as shocked by that as she thought she would be. Twenty-seven years and she'd been with one man in all that time. Arthur had been an old friend from out of town who'd come through on a road trip. The relationship had only lasted about a half year before they'd called it quits. It'd been a long-distance thing, with her in Pine Junction and him in Phoenix, but when he'd accidentally sent her an amorous email that had clearly been meant for someone else—the inclusion of the name "Karla" had been a pretty good tip-off about that—the relationship had been doomed.

Candace lowered her voice even more. "Come on, Nic, I know you've had a teeny bit of experience in… things."

"Not *that* sort of experience." She may have read a lot of romances, but she was smart enough to know that her life wasn't one of them—even if she wished it was. "You know I've never been all that adventurous."

"Again…if you just had the *chance.*" Candace tilted her head, the feathers in her hair blowing under the ceiling fan. "Especially with—"

"Don't say it again, Candy—"

"Shane." Candace grinned.

Nicki gave up, knowing that when Candace was on a roll, she was on a roll. "Sure. If I found myself in a dark room with Shane Carter and I had the chance, I'd do what any red-blooded girl would do. Satisfied?"

Her jittering pulse must've been obvious to anyone within sight.

"Adventurous," Candace said, patting Nicki's shoulder just before the band took the stage. "I like that."

Then Candace started clapping and whooping, welcoming the players.

"Rock and roll!" Candace said over her bare shoulder, winking at Nicki while she left.

And there was no doubt she was going to have the time of her life as she sashayed toward the dance floor.

After Candace whispered in the lead guitarist's ear, he slid a grin to her.

Next thing Nicki knew, the band had ripped into a Def Leppard song and Candace was dancing in the middle of the floor, luring just about every male eye in the county.

Nicki took the opportunity to commune with her beer. Another sip, the coolness slipping down her throat, spreading warmth as she kept scanning the room. For a minute she forgot all about tomorrow's meeting with the corporate rep and let her mind wander to what Candace had been talking about.

What *would* it be like to let herself go?

The more the music played, the more Nicki reveled in the corset pushing up her breasts, hugging her waist. The more she could imagine a man's fingers undoing the lacings…

Fantasy.

It kicked in as she imagined a cowboy coming into a Western bar through the half-doors, the dusty street shadowed behind him, leaving him in tall, rugged silhouette as he stood in the entrance, finding her with his gaze.

A gaze that looked like Shane's…*always*.

Her tummy flipped as she imagined the thud of his boots on the planked floor, the way his steps would slow as he approached her….

The song ended and everyone applauded, bringing Nicki back to rights.

She drank more beer, intending to put this fire out.

And that's when she saw him.

An actual tall man sauntering into the room, a black cowboy hat set low over his brow, showing only a strong chin and full lips. An outlaw, from his long-sleeved shirt and his dark vest and jeans, to the silver-tipped black leather of his boots. Lean and mean. Just below his cocky grin, a kerchief bunched, as if he was ready to go out and rob a train, just like Jesse James.

Heat trailed from Nicki's chest and downward, through her belly, spreading even lower than that as she felt a pitter-pat between her legs.

How would he react if she wandered away from the safety of the bar to get herself into his line of sight?

As the band took up an old standard—"Slow Ride"— the outlaw ambled toward a group of town girls dressed as Playboy bunnies and buxom cheerleaders. They welcomed him with smiles and giggles while he hooked his thumbs into his belt loops, as if they'd already met him.

Was he visiting someone in Pine Junction? Or was he a new ranch hand on one of the spreads and Nicki hadn't seen him in town yet?

The corset pressed against her breasts, reminding her that they were more on display than she'd ever allowed before. But you know what? Her breasts did look pretty good, if she said so herself.

She watched the outlaw flash a hot-as-all-get-out smile to his harem of women. One of them stood on her tiptoes and stole his hat from his head, leaving his dirty-blond hair ruffled. His playful smile sent the contingent of fools into more laughter, and it did something foolish to Nicki, too.

A sharp ache settled in her sex, pounding.

He kept smiling, and something familiar knocked at her chest.

A reassuring smile she'd seen years and years ago,

just before a boy had helped her to her feet, her body still smarting from the breath-jarring fall she'd taken from the fence.

The hero underneath the bad-boy reputation.

Shane Carter—and he was all man now.

As if he felt her watching him, he caught her gaze, sending that piercing heat between her legs to a twist of agony. When he tipped his hat to her, Nicki wondered if he recognized the cowgirl next door, or if all he saw was...

A saloon girl.

A sex goddess who was making him grin as he swept an appreciative glance over her.

When she turned back around to the bar, she almost dropped her beer. Her hands were shaking because of the adrenaline rush, the tremors in her belly.

She'd been, what, fifteen when he'd left? Then his father had passed on from that heart attack around the time her own parents had died, and Shane's older brother, Tommy, had run the Slanted C. Supposedly, ever since then, Shane had been somewhere in the vicinity of Dallas, working on some cutting horse ranch.

But he was back now.

And, from the looks of it, he was painting the town red, just as she would've expected the rebellious son of the Slanted C to do.

Maybe connecting gazes with him had thrown Nicki for a loop, because her heart was beating like the drums in the wild country song that the band was now playing. *Bang, bang, bang.* She tried not to think about the breadth of his shoulders under that dark shirt, his waist tapering into lean hips, the long legs ending in those bad boy boots.

Then again, maybe his appeal was just in the costume. Maybe she was just thinking too much about those fantasies Candace had been talking about.

Nicki's body pitter-patted again, demanding that she turn around to look at him one more time.

But when she heard a deep voice right behind her, she startled, surprise jabbing her all over.

"Look who's all dressed up."

A low, dark drawl.

When Nicki glanced over her shoulder, he was there, so close that she could see the stubble emerging on his cheeks and jawline and smell the lime of the shaving cream he must've used.

He was near enough that Nicki could also see the slight cleft in his chin, the dark blue of eyes that boasted lashes that had no right to be on a man.

Her stomach lifted and then somersaulted. A foreign feeling, like it'd never happened to her before. Or as if it'd never happened with this kind of force.

"You recognized me?" she asked loudly, over the music. Somehow, she sounded just like a saloon girl, a little too saucy, a lot interested.

"Sure I recognized you," he said over the song.

Then, to her shock, he reached out, touched a curl that had sprung from her upswept hairdo. Near his fingers, the skin on her neck tingled, sending a shower of awareness over her chest, through her belly, ending in an even more intense drill of lust below the belt.

He added, "No one's got hair like this."

He let go of her root beer–colored curl, even though it seemed as if he didn't really want to.

Or was she imagining that?

"So…" she said over the band's music.

He had to take off his hat, then lean in to hear, and the intimacy kept her body thudding and bumping. Damn, he smelled good, like he'd just gotten out of the shower. Her lips throbbed from being so close to his cheek.

"You're back on the ranch?" she added.

He nodded, turning his face toward her so he could answer. When he spoke, he warmed her ear, making her realize that his mouth was only a kiss away.

"Tommy recently left with his family for greener pastures with his wife's family in east Texas," he said. "And my mom's off visiting my aunt in Oklahoma for a while."

"You've taken over?"

"I suppose I have."

He sounded amused by the turn of events, but something in his tone also hinted of a darker reason for his return to Pine Junction.

But before she could ask about that, he'd already gone back to being that outlaw, one thumb hooked through a belt loop, his gaze lowered as he moved to speak in her ear again.

"Rumor has it that *you're* looking to do business with an out-of-towner."

Something took a nosedive in her chest. This didn't sound like flirting any more.

"A neighbor's business is always my business," he said, "especially if it concerns the introduction of dudes."

Definitely not flirting.

So much for fantasy. Shane Carter had come across the room to merely talk business to his next-door neighbor.

And you know what? It made Nicki bristle, because she knew that, in his eyes, she still had to be the little-sister type to him, the girl in pigtails he'd protected from his father's anger once upon a time.

That wasn't her anymore, especially tonight of all nights.

"Do you think city people are going to pollute Pine Junction?" she asked. "Is that what you're afraid of, Carter?"

"I have my concerns, seeing as your land borders my family's. Do you have any idea how selling out to a dude operation is going to change the tenor of the town?"

Selling out. That stung, mostly because she *had* thought good and hard about it. But, the truth was, plenty of Pine Junction's citizens were just as hard up for money as she was. In fact, she was in competition with some of the other ranches for the investment firm's favor, and their representative would be making visits to some of their spreads, too.

"Is that why you came back?" she asked, leveling her tone. "To make sure a dude resort won't cheapen Pine Junction with spas and four-star restaurants?"

"That's one among many reasons."

His jaw had gone tight. Her heartbeat punched up, and hyperactive butterflies flew through her belly.

Then he ran another long gaze down Nicki, as if taking a different view of her.

Her skin flamed as his slow gaze turned into something much more, roaming right back up her body, leaving a trail of tingling, addictive shivers in his wake.

Nicki's sex clenched, priming itself for something it hadn't had in a long time.

The tingles blazed upward, sending prickles of heat through her—like flames eating their way out from under her skin. Beneath her bodice, her nipples went sensitive, peaking, and she wanted to be touched as thoroughly as she'd been looked at.

Then Shane raised an eyebrow, as if she'd totally misinterpreted his glance, and her reverie shattered into a thousand heartbreaking pieces.

This wasn't a fantasy at all, and that's what she'd always been afraid of with Shane.

2

As NICKI WADE WALKED away from Shane, he almost stopped her.

Almost.

When Shane had first seen her across the room, he hadn't actually recognized her. His body had only reacted to a punch of lust straight to the gut at the sight of a slender, toned woman in a sexy dress, her curls swept up into a bohemian mass, one corkscrew escaping to tickle a long, seductive neck.

He hadn't been able to glance away, his groin thudding with every kick of his pulse.

Then…

Then he'd seen little Nicki Wade under the surface.

Nicki, who used to wear that crazy hair of hers in pigtails…until one day.

Shane remembered something now—a time just before he'd left Pine Junction. A day when he'd done a double take at her.

She'd been with her friends at the annual spring rodeo, and it'd been the first time he'd seen her with her hair down. A glimpse of who she'd be one day set off a burst of attraction in him that he'd quickly tamped down. After all, she was Nicki Wade and she was fifteen, way too young for a guy on the edge of graduation—a guy who spent too much time being watched by the sheriff because of drag racing and hell raising.

A guy too fast for a sweet girl like her.

He'd forgotten all about that until now. But it didn't matter so much. Shane would be damned if he didn't tell her what he thought about getting too cozy with that skunk of a business that had contacted him just this morning about his own family ranch, the Slanted C.

Shane had laughed off the representative, a man named Russell Alexander. What made Alexander think that the Carters would be interested in converting their spread into a dude resort? The businessman hadn't come right out and said it, but Shane had the feeling the guy knew that the Slanted C was in just as much trouble as the Square W+W.

And here Shane had thought he'd been doing so well in hiding that fact. No one in town realized just how far Tommy and his idiotic get-rich-quick investments had put the ranch in jeopardy. To make matters worse, the recession had taken every penny Shane had in savings, and his family was already in loans up to their necks— not that he'd ever let anyone know. If there was one thing Shane had always been, it was proud, and he knew he could be more of a man than his dad or Tommy; *he* would be the one to get the Slanted C turned around. But he would also do it for his mom's sake, since the ranch had come from her side of the family and he was bound and determined to make sure she had the home she'd grown up in and loved for the rest of her life.

And he wasn't about to go dude to accomplish any of that.

He could almost hear his father browbeating him because, somehow, he would've found a way to blame Shane for this entire mess: *Didn't I teach you any business sense, you moron? Don't you have one lick of smarts in that head of yours?*

Tommy's part in it wouldn't have mattered: Shane was the one whom his dad expected to help out on the ranch, like any good son. And Barry Carter would've probably even ignored how Shane's older brother had left Pine Junction with his tail between his legs, retreating to his wife's family for some support.

Maybe Shane was just meant to take the brunt of everything, as he'd done whenever Dad let his anger get the better of him with Mom. Taking the brunt back then had been instinctive, a protective urge that he'd hidden well from most everyone except his family.

It hadn't been anyone's business but the Carters', anyway, yet taking the brunt had forged him into a man early.

Very early.

His gaze was still on Nicki as she wove through a crowd of cowboys, away from him.

Yeah, he was sorry, so then why couldn't he just come out and say that he'd projected his disappointment in himself onto her? Why couldn't he admit that he hated that he'd actually been *entertaining* the thought of accepting Russell Alexander's interest in the Slanted C, even though it made him feel beaten?

Because Shane couldn't admit that he was down before the fight had even begun, couldn't allow everyone to already see him for the failure his father had always accused him of being.

The band had paused in their song list, and the lead singer apologized, saying they had a broken guitar string. He chattered to the crowd about all the costumes he saw in the room while they waited for a replacement guitar.

Shane knew it was now or never with Nicki. Damn it, she was his neighbor, and he couldn't let things stand as they were, so he caught up to her at the side of the band's stage.

"Nicki…"

It was obvious that she'd been stewing on their conversation, and she launched into another question right away.

"Just why are you back in Pine Junction, Carter?"

Her light green eyes were filled with anger, and somehow, he was responding to that passion, a thrust of need bolting straight to his cock.

But this was Nicki Wade. What did his cock have to do with it?

A girl like her wouldn't like it temporary and wild, and that was just how *he* always wanted it—without strings or commitment. You couldn't get freedom in a relationship, and he'd never been the type for one of those, anyway. Not after what he'd seen his mom go through with his dad.

Nicki kept at him. "You can't come back into town and start passing judgment on those of us who've gone through the ups and downs of living here."

"You're right."

He didn't tell her why he'd left, though. There was no reason for him to explain the reasons he'd run off, because that last day with his father had been the point of no return. He'd finally hit the man back while defending his mom, and she'd had no choice but to ask Shane to leave.

"He's much easier to live with when you're not here," she'd said, brokenhearted at the choice she'd been forced to make.

And Shane had gone, just as broken, himself.

"I apologize, Nicki." He paused, then added, "And I'm sorry about your parents, too—the car accident. They were good people."

He'd admired her family and how they were so loving that they even embraced their employees as their own. Shane had never had that. Not even close.

She looked just like he did most mornings in the mirror: at the end of her rope, having gone through every possible idea to keep the family legacy running strong.

As she took in his apology, she nodded stiffly.

It was beyond him to go away with her in such a state. "I just keep seeing the little girl on the W+W riding around on her first pony near our property lines. And I don't want her to get hurt by a huge corporation like the one that's coming into our midst tomorrow."

Even under her tanned skin, she seemed to blanch.

Somehow he'd offended her again.

"You think I can't handle some businessman? You still believe I'm some little girl who…?"

"Hey, I didn't mean to say—"

Her voice took on some steel. "You really don't know much about me at all, do you?"

With that, she turned around, leaving him near the stage.

He watched her walk away. Hips. Skin. Heat on a hot autumn night.

And Shane kept watching her until he had to shake himself out of it. He shouldn't be thinking about Nicki Wade.

He shouldn't be thinking about anything other than every woman in the room who might like to spend some time with an outlaw tonight in a hideaway, where he could forget just about everything else for a few precious hours.

How COULD SHANE CARTER just amble back into town and rile her up like this?

God, all Nicki wanted to do was show him he was wrong...and to make him see *her*.

Every bit of the woman she had become while he'd been away.

She watched how the girls in the room—brides, dark seductresses, even a slave Princess Leia—gravitated toward Shane now. It was just as it'd always been with him—he moved toward the edges of the dance floor but stayed off of it altogether, as if outlaws *never* danced.

Whatever the case, she didn't want to stand around until he inevitably changed his mind and scooped a girl into his arms, making his choice for the night. Even picturing him with another woman turned her stomach.

Why, though? What was he to her?

Nicki made her way across the room, to where her ride, Manny, was raiding the buffet table, stacking biscuits, cornbread and cookies into a network of large paper napkins.

"Hey, Manny."

Her thirtysomething ranch foreman turned around,

offering a gap-toothed smile. It complemented his "costume," which consisted of him sticking some straw into his beat-up Stetson and calling himself a "scarecrow."

Nicki glanced at his overloaded napkins. "I'm ready to go home whenever you are."

"Any time," he said, grabbing another stack of corn bread and piling it on the rest. "Just came here for the grub, anyway."

"Thanks, Manny." She would leave a message on Candace's cell phone to tell her she'd left. Candace had planned to stop drinking after one champagne and drive their pickup home, anyway, so it wasn't as if Nicki was stranding her.

She could tell that Manny was trying not to check out her costume, but he sure had a bit of a brotherly frown on his face. Any employee on the ranch would probably be doing the same if they saw her, and Nicki just wanted to get out of sight before too many got the opportunity.

Manny fetched a couple of beers from an ice-filled aluminum tub for good measure and stuck them under his armpits before they left the ballroom, going out of the Grand Hotel's Old West lobby, with its scarred cherry wood furnishings and oil portraits of the town's founding fathers.

After finding his blue pickup, which featured cloudy areas where the paint had faded, they hopped in. Nicki left that message with Candace on her voice mail, telling her that she would be waiting up with the company of a good book in her room if there was anything exciting to talk about.

Soon enough, she and Manny were at her two-level colonial ranch house that had seen much better days, its white facade in need of paint just as much as Manny's truck.

Nicki hugged him good-night then got out. The porch protested under her footsteps as he drove away toward the employee cabins.

She went to her second-floor room, realizing that she was tired—too tired to even read or wait up for Candace. Not bothering to turn on the lights before taking off her ankle-high saloon girl boots, she fell forward onto the bed.

Resting her forehead on her arms, she started to chide herself for leaving the party. What she should've done was stayed, showing Shane Carter that a mild confrontation with him wouldn't ruin her night, even if it had.

Damn it—she and those books. She and those *dreams*. What was it about Shane that had the power to resurrect them tonight? Books were supposed to let her escape, not bring everything into crummy focus.

Her mind couldn't stop meandering back to Shane in that outlaw outfit, though. To make matters worse, her anger at him boiled her blood even now, heating her up in a way she didn't want.

Even so, she ached, deep in her belly. She felt the needled pressure of desire between her legs, just from picturing him as that long, tall shadow in the saloon doors, pausing there as he saw his saloon girl waiting by the bar.

Wrong. So wrong to think about him like this.

But the wrongness made her want to do it all the more, and she remembered how he'd looked at her across the room, the first time he'd seen her tonight.

How she'd sworn that he'd been stripping off her dress with his gaze, piece by piece.

And then he'd looked again after they'd been talking; slowly, with a languid visual caress that had felt as good as anything physical.

Scorched by the thought, Nicki rolled to her back and raised her arms over her head, holding to the memory of those long glances, feeling them stroke her.

Shane *had* wanted her, if only for a moment. And in that fleeting time, she hadn't been that cowgirl next door. She'd been someone entirely different—more powerful, holding the reins.

Nicki stared toward the ceiling; she could see the white expanse of it in the darkness. She should've tested Shane, should've found out if he would've responded to an overture from her. But in her mind…

Well, in her mind she could make sure that he *did* want her, couldn't she? In her mind, she could have it any way she wanted it.

Outside, the wind flirted with the shutters and hushed through the half-opened window. She closed her eyes, picturing the outlaw in her head, and her body hummed. As she breathed, her dress whisked against the covers, a soft, sensual sound.

Shane…

No one would know if she touched herself right now, pretending it was him. She was here, alone.

No one would ever know.

She ran one hand down her neck, over a breast, which felt round and ripe under her palm. Sexy under the satin. Tracing the outline of it, she thought of him.

I'm sorry for what I said back at the party, he would tell her if he was here now.

But she would quiet him right up, arching under his hand, just as she was doing now. She would urge him to undo her corset.

Nicki pulled on one of the lacings, trying not to think about the reality, the chances she would be taking by opening herself up and letting an actual man do this.

As she opened the corset, fantasy enveloped her, the air breathing over her exposed skin.

What would he say if he saw her like this?

What would he *do?*

She pictured Shane's face with the bandanna covering the lower half of it.

The outlaw. The bad boy who had a chance for redemption...

Feeling free, she slid her hand lower, pushing up her dress and pressing against her sex, pretending it was his hand. She rocked her hips slightly, pressing harder, circling her fingers over her clit.

He was the one stroking her, his face hidden by that bandanna as well as the night that swallowed her room.

Give me everything, he would say in an almost unrecognizable voice.

Nicki pressed harder, faster. Her panties were getting damp now, wetter and wetter as the outlaw made the sexual steam rise inside her, pulsing. Throbbing.

She groaned. "What do you want?"

Her money? Her life?

In her fantasy, he pushed a finger into her, and she bucked. Higher and higher, darker and darker as her fantasy swirled, sucking her in.

I just want you, he would say and, this time, it *was* Shane's voice.

Higher, harder...

Nicki came with an inner bang, like a gunshot that echoed and echoed through her, her breathing choppy as she opened her eyes back to the present.

The quiet of the house.

The disturbed covers on her bed.

The moon-shaded corners of her room.

It was a while before she rolled to her stomach again and fell asleep, but when she did, she went back to dreaming of the outlaw and what he would do to her next.

BACK AT THE PARTY, Candace had been shaking her booty on the dance floor, yippy-yo-kay-yaying with every cowboy who was game.

But she hadn't been so into her fun that she'd completely forgotten about Nicki—especially when her cousin had left the ballroom with Manny the foreman.

Now, as Candace stood in the hallway of the hotel, her cell phone to her ear, she listened to the voice mail.

"Don't kill me," Nicki said, "but I'm exhausted, Candy. I had a great time while I was there, but I'm going home. I'll be waiting up for you in my room with one of those 'adventurous books' so you can tell me about your big night. That is, if you even come home. Anyway, we'll do this again soon—I promise. It's just that…"

Nicki hadn't needed to mention the big day tomorrow, because Candace had already guessed that it would be the supposed reason Nicki had left.

But Candace had another theory.

She tucked the phone into a holster that hung from one hip and sauntered to the door of the party, where the band was winding up a Garth Brooks song. As they dove into the last notes and then announced another break, Candace found Shane Carter, standing at a table, the focal point of three giggling women.

The Don Juan of Pine Junction.

Easy guys didn't interest her, and that's how most of the men here seemed. Way too easy. So when Candace narrowed her gaze at Shane, it wasn't because she was zooming in on him for herself.

Earlier, Nicki had been engaged in quite the discussion with him, and it looked as if it hadn't been a good, flirty chat, either. Nicki had deserted the talk with a crushed look on her face, and it had torn at Candace just as strongly.

All women knew what it was like to be crushed by a crush, and Nicki was more sensitive than most. Beneath all the straight-talk and confidence in her work, Nicki was still finding herself, and it hadn't been easy while being sheltered by that ranch all these years. Candace had always taken great pleasure in getting Nicki out and about, even as a kid, and she'd seen Nicki blossom when she wasn't acting like a girl who'd taken on so much responsibility with the ranch much too early.

It broke Candace's heart to think that Nicki might never get the joy that was to be taken out of life. Even Candace, who'd had her share of hard times lately, knew that there was still fun to be had, even during the worst of it.

Besides, hadn't Nicki said that she'd be in to using that saloon girl costume?

Candace went to the quiet lobby, asked a desk clerk for a pen and paper, then scribbled.

If you're up to it, how about coming over at about 10:00 tonight? I'm in my room, on my bed,

waiting to see if you'll be here. Waiting for an
outlaw to break out of his cell and be with me,
his woman, the saloon girl with the fishnet stockings and garters.

Had she overdone it? It sounded like something from
Nicki's books—novels that Candace had also become
addicted to over the years.

Okay, maybe it was over the top, but if a known
playboy like Shane was to be lured to Nicki, an invitation would have to have some spice. Sure, Nicki would
be in bed reading, as she'd said on her phone message,
but if Shane showed up, she could always tell him to
get out. Or she could tell him to stay. And, from the
way Candace had seen Shane devouring Nicki with his
gaze earlier, she had no doubts that he would agree to
whatever Nicki decided.

She ended the note by adding the address of the
Wade house, mentioning that his saloon girl would be
in the first bedroom on the second floor.

Nicki's room.

One last niggle made Candace hesitate, but she told
herself that all Nicki needed was opportunity. Hadn't
she admitted earlier that if the chance came along, she'd
hop on it?

Yes, she had. Besides, Nicki needed this—confidence and, more important, some darned fun.

Candace went back to the ballroom, waiting until
Shane ambled over to the bar for a drink, then marched
right up to him before any other women could waylay
him.

"Hi, Shane," she said, friendly as any old fairy god-
mother. Or madam.

When he turned around, he didn't greet her with any kind of playboy's "how do you do," as she expected he might. No, at the sight of her, he might've even been a little…wary.

"Candace," he said, offering his hand for a shake. "Nicki's cousin, right? Haven't seen you for a good while."

"I'm on an extended visit." The circumstances of the visit—getting fired, having trouble getting rehired anywhere—stayed buried in her, deep and low, where embarrassment covered them.

He leaned back against the bar, and she couldn't help but notice that he was checking out the room.

"Looking for Nicki?" she asked.

"Nope."

"Well, that's good, because she left already. I think you ruffled her feathers."

He frowned. "I didn't mean to. We had a few words about that corporate guy coming out to her ranch tomorrow, and… Hell, the conversation just didn't end the way I hoped it would."

So Candace had been right about them having some sort of tiff.

As he lifted his beer to take a drink, she went for it, tucking the note she'd written into a pocket in his vest.

"If you want to make amends with Nicki, this is how to do it." She got a little bolder, praying that the end would justify the means. "Nicki's a pretty shy person. You know that, right?"

"She wasn't shy while she was putting me in my place."

"That's true. When Nicki's wound up, Nicki's wound up." Candace took a breath. Here it went. "Before she left, she was still on fire, and I suggested she put that to good use. That's when she wrote this."

He glanced at the paper peeking out of his vest. "Wrote what, exactly?"

He said it as if he were definitely interested. This was totally going to work.

"You've got to read it to see," Candace said, lifting an eyebrow, knowing that she'd done what she could to hook Shane Carter's attention and make Nicki's night.

And maybe even her decade.

Candace sauntered away, hoping Shane would read that note soon, then show up at Nicki's bedroom tonight, giving her the best apology *ever*.

3

SHANE RETRIEVED the note from his pocket shortly after Candace had gone back to the dance floor, and after he read it, he couldn't believe it.

Meet Nicki at the Wade house?

Nicki?

After their argument, he wasn't sure what to think.

Then he remembered how she'd looked at him at first, just as any woman looked at a man. And that costume she was wearing...

Nicki really *had* grown up.

Had her anger with him only been a prelude to more? He'd known women like that in the past—ones who liked to argue as foreplay.

Maybe Nicki was the same. He had a note right here in his hand to suggest it.

He glanced at his old watch. Twenty minutes till ten, the meeting hour.

Hell, if a woman wanted him to come over, he wasn't about to say no. First of all, there'd been an undeniable attraction between them from the start, setting off sparks as they'd talked to each other, angry or not.

Besides that, he was used to cleansing his mind with sex, and Lord knew he needed to forget about everything that'd been waiting here for him in Pine Junction on the Slanted C.

In the end, an invitation was an invitation, right? Even if it was from the girl next door.

It just went to show that nothing ever stayed the same, so who was he to deny her?

Blanking his mind to any mental arguments, he left the hotel and walked to Main Street, where he'd parked his Dodge truck. The gas lamps lent a timeless atmosphere to the night, along with the Old West facades of Pine Junction—some of which had been used as Hollywood sets, back in the day. Planked sidewalks, saloons and rising hills that led to an abandoned silver mine gave him reason to get in the mood for this outlaw-meets-saloon-girl date.

All the while, he kept thinking of Nicki in that costume, Nicki heating him from boot to hat with just a long look when she first saw him...

Nicki's surprising invitation.

As he drove to the W+W, the faint moonlight painted the white fences along the dirt road that led to the ranch. When he got there, he parked near a copse of pine trees, far out of the open.

Before leaving the truck, he checked his cell phone. A few minutes to ten. She had to be waiting.

All he kept seeing was Nicki Wade's light green eyes and how they'd heated him up with the fire in them.

But then his conscience came rushing back. Nicki's dad, who'd been downright friendly and courteous to Shane when a whole lot of people in Pine Junction hadn't been, might not have appreciated this. There'd been too many older, well-played daughters around the area for Shane to have been the father favorite. Nicki had been so young that there was no doubt her dad had felt secure in the knowledge that he wouldn't be dealing with Shane in that way for a good, long while, if ever.

But Nicki was able to make her *own* decisions now, and she had asked him over.

Another look at the time told Shane that it was ten o'clock on the nose.

He got out of the truck, took care with closing the door, then walked the rest of the way to the house, where the entrance had been left unlocked.

Opening it, he crossed the threshold, into a hallway just off a well-used parlor where the Wades used to greet their guests. He'd been in the room, with its tarnished crystal lamps and old velvet sofas, only a few times, during neighborly parties when he'd been a kid, eager to leave and run around outside where his parents and big brother couldn't keep an eye on him. Nicki had been much the same—fidgety while the adults had sat around and talked, her ill-fitting dresses always askew before the first hour was up, even though she hadn't been doing much. Just sitting on a couch had seemed to be enough to put her in a state of dishabille.

She'd been cute, he recalled, but she'd been a sweet kind of cute. The kind that went against the nature of the bachelor he'd eventually become—one who'd seen how miserable his mother had been during marriage and decided that it wasn't for him.

Second floor, she had written.

He quietly mounted the stairs, freezing every time a creak sounded under his feet. His pulse thumped, competing with the grandfather clock in the parlor. Both sounds seemed to flood the house.

When he'd finished with the steps, he moved toward the only room that had its door closed, then rested his hand on the old-fashioned crystal knob, turning it.

Inside, the darkness was cut only by a sliver of moonlight from the gaping curtains. It was enough to show him the lower half of the bed, where his saloon girl rested. She lay facedown, her dress gathered near her hips in a bunch of satin, her long legs still encased in the fishnet pattern of her stockings.

He heard breathing, even and soft.

Nicki—she hadn't been kidding with that note.

Waiting for my outlaw to break out of his cell and be with me, his woman, the saloon girl with the fishnet stockings and garters...

But had she already fallen asleep?

Well, yeah. *That'd* make sense with the scenario in the note. The outlaw coming back to his hideaway and finding the saloon girl in his bed, waiting for him.

Someone who'd allow him a little escapade, just for a night, he reminded himself.

He pulled up the bandanna over the lower half of his face and moved to the bed. He heard her sigh, then shift restlessly in a rustle of that maddeningly alluring dress.

Yup, he was a bad, bad man on the run from the law, and he was going to show this woman just how dangerous meeting with him could be.

He went to the foot of the mattress, rested his hands on her stocking-covered ankles. Warm under the silk. Delicate.

Easing his hands higher, he coasted his thumbs over her calves.

She sighed again, wiggling her hips.

Lust, pure and simple, bolted through Shane, making his cock hard, and he moved his hands higher, over the backs of her knees, over her thighs, where her stockings ended and garters began.

He heard her breathing hitch, and he knew the game was really on now.

And if this was how Nicki wanted it, he was ready to play it.

"Don't make a sound," the outlaw whispered, reaching under her dress. "Not a word…"

IN THE HAZE OF A DREAM—the aftermath of the fantasy she'd had before drifting off to sleep, one that seemed incredibly real—Nicki felt the outlaw's hands on her rear end, cupping her.

Don't make a sound. And she didn't as her face rubbed against the bedcovers, her hands pressed against the mattress. Her breasts were flattened beneath her, making them feel swollen, raw against the quilting.

In that foggy dream, she felt the bed dip as the bandit climbed onto it, heard the box springs creak. His legs brushed the outside of hers as he straddled her.

"You're probably wondering why I'm here," he said in a deep Western drawl, a whisper above the stillness of the night.

She moaned in answer.

He slipped his hands—big, work-roughened hands—from her butt to her hips, then…

Oh, then underneath, to her belly.

Her muscles there jumped, and the tiny flinches

made her gasp. Desire nipped at her skin, and she felt plumped, aching, slippery. Ready already.

He spoke again, rough and ready, too. "You knew this is the only place I can hide out. You waited for me."

A hunted man, she thought. A fugitive from the law. Dangerous.

And he sounded just like Shane.

That revved her up even more in her dream-state, and she lifted her hips, knowing he was tender and gentle underneath his dangerous exterior. Her fantasy man took that as a sign to go on, coaxing his hands into her undies.

She muffled her moan.

He laughed, low and lethal, easing a finger between her slick folds, urging her legs apart. Down, up, circling her clit, taking up where they'd left off before. Her hips moved with his strokes, especially when he used his other hand to pull her back to him, nestling her rear end against him.

Her fantasy man was hard. She could feel the ridge of him even through his pants and the cotton of her undies.

Panting, she felt her breath, moist and hot, against the covers. She was still in a fever dream, a million miles away from the Nicki she'd always known.

Grinding back against him, she made him moan, too, his hands grasping her hips as he encouraged her to go on, harder. Slower.

The feel of him… Even in a dream, the primal need hit her hard. Damn it, she wanted him inside her without *anything* between them.

He coasted his finger up and into her, just like earlier, when she'd touched herself and exploded by just thinking about him. But this time it was better, more intense.

He swept his finger around while using his palm to press against her clit. She couldn't do anything but make little helpless sounds, couldn't even find her voice so she could tell him that this wasn't enough. She wanted it all.

She rocked against him, every cell in her body palpitating, stomping in an all-consuming rhythm that beat on her damp skin, in her ears, in her temples. There was a pressure in her that she'd never felt before—a rising joy that she rode up and up.

"There," he said on a near growl. He churned his erection against her, echoing the sinuous movement with his hand on her sex...*in* her sex. "You like it bad, don't you?"

Yes, she did.

She was getting so high that she didn't think she could go any further, her body tight, ready to fly open. And, when he snuck his other hand to her clit again, working it until she couldn't stand another second, she broke.

Bursting apart, pieces of her all around, in the air, tumbling, trying to find a place to fit together again during this freefall.

Showering like rain.

A storm.

A banging, breath-stealing push of shudders as she fell back to the bed, crying out against the mattress as he covered her mouth with his hand.

As Nicki sucked in breath upon breath against his skin, she opened her eyes part way, still in the dream.

But...

She blinked.

Calluses on his hand. The taste of skin—musky, male.

The hint of her juices on him, too.

The voice of the outlaw again. "You don't know what kind of danger you've put yourself in, waiting here for me."

The voice…this voice.

Shane's.

She blinked. Held her breath as reality rushed her.

Real. This was actually happening.

Her heart blipped like a series of beeps counting down to a gasp that wouldn't come. It was so dark that she couldn't see much else but the cut of moonlight slashing across the foot of her bed.

His whispers seemed to weave themselves into the surreal, carnal shadows.

"Not a word," he said, tracing her mouth with a finger, clearly intending to continue what he'd started.

Lust fireworked through her. *Had* he wanted her so much at the party that he'd come here, just like the bad boy he'd always been?

Had that look he'd first given her from across the room said everything?

Heart exploding, she turned around to him, and even in the near darkness, she found him with a bandanna over the lower half of his face. With her free hand, she tugged it down. Her pulse kicked in her ears, her blood going through her so fast that it felt like lightning.

"Shane?" she whispered, although she couldn't see much of his face.

He froze for some reason.

She didn't move, either. She wasn't sure why—

maybe because this had started out as a dream. She'd been half-asleep, but at some point, she'd been awake.

So, so awake.

Dreaming had only been an excuse for her to throw herself into her biggest desire, and it was just now enveloping her with that reality.

Even so, her pulse chugged along, propelled by the possibility that he had wanted this as much as she had.

But when he spoke, he blasted her world apart.

"Who else would it be but me?" he asked.

For a second, she followed the echo of his question, the reverberations chipping away at her.

Nicki grabbed her blankets to cover herself and snapped on a bedside light.

And there he sat, the outlaw Shane, shock registering on his face, too, as he saw that this wasn't the welcome he'd been expecting.

It took Shane a few seconds to come to terms with what was happening.

Why did she seem so flabbergasted?

But there she was, huddled under the bedcovers, her hair a tumble of falling curls and one lone feather that had stayed in during all the excitement. The few others were spread over the bed, like the aftermath of some crash.

The flush of her cheeks made the green of her eyes stand out in surprised fervor.

But why was she reacting like this if she'd invited him over?

Shane got up off the bed, thankful that his untucked shirt covered all evidence of his arousal. Not that she wouldn't know his state, but...

Ah, crap.

"The note…" He lowered his voice. "You wrote me a note."

"What?"

Now he was really confused. He dug into his jeans pocket where he'd stored the paper, then offered it to her.

She read it, her brow furrowed. She looked adorable, even if she was likely to murder him any moment.

His body was still pounding from everything that'd just gone on in that bed.

Nicki Wade. She'd been *dressed* as a saloon girl, as if it was a comfortable thing for her, but then again, outside of costumes, he'd never thought that Nicki would be so…

He couldn't come up with a word that described what she'd conjured up in him. All he knew was that he'd wanted her more than anything now. She was perfect—her scent, like fresh summer grass; her smooth skin; the way she'd fit in his hands; the gasps and moans that had reached right into him, twisting and turning until he was so wound up that it hurt to stand here staring at her.

It felt as if she'd always been here, waiting.

"What the hell is this?" she finally said in her own edged whisper as she held that note.

Either Nicki was playing the innocent or she was truly flummoxed. He was going to go with the latter.

"Candace," he said, thinking that he should've known better. "She must've been setting us up. She wrote that note and put it in my pocket."

Nicki was already out of the bed, the covers wrapped

around her, even though she still had most of her clothing on. She picked up a TV remote from her nightstand.

"Nic—" he started to say.

She threw it at him and he dodged. At the same time, he scooped his hat off the floor.

"Can we be civilized about this?" he asked.

"Civilized?" Even their harsh whispers seemed to rock the house. "This is beyond civil."

She searched her nightstand for something else to throw, and he darted over to her before she could destroy her entire room.

He'd clasped one of her wrists in his hand, and he could swear that his skin against hers set them both to sizzling.

His cock gave an agonizing thud, so he let go of her and she backed away, as if rocked hard, too.

"I understand why you're upset."

"Just what do you think I am, for you to come over here and…?"

He offered a grin—one that usually got him out of scrapes—and shrugged.

Cheeks flushing even more, she tightened the covers around her, but that only served to push up her breasts. Every move she made echoed in his groin, which was still pounding, killing him.

Nicki made a "come on" gesture with her fingers, so he prepared to explain it all.

"When a woman invites a man in," he said, "it's hard for him to say no. I took the note at face value."

"But I didn't invite you here."

"By God, Nicki, I'm sorry."

Her chest kept heaving, her skin going redder.

Then it hit him. Nicki hadn't exactly kicked him out

of bed right away, even though she hadn't been expecting a man to sneak up on her in costume. In fact, it'd been quite a spell before she'd come out of the whole scenario.

"Nicki," he said softly, "even if you didn't write that note, did you want me to come here?"

She made as if she were going to grab the pillow from the bed and throw it at him, but then she stopped and plopped down on the mattress.

He'd hit a target, and it was as if the bull's-eye was ringing in him, too.

"Listen," he said, "if you'd told me at any time to get out, I would've."

"I was half-asleep when it all started."

That made him feel even worse, and she must've seen it in the way he wiped a hand over his face.

"Nicki…"

"No." She sighed. "Jeez, I actually believe you when you say that being here was a mistake."

The way she said "mistake"…

Tentatively, he came nearer to the bed. "When I found you sleeping, I thought it was a part of the act suggested in that note."

When she looked up at him with those big green eyes, his heart almost broke. There was something he couldn't figure out, almost as if he was hurting her by explaining everything.

Nicki gestured toward the door again, as if trying to avoid the same questions he was struggling with. "The door's waiting for you."

Dismissed, just as so many others had done to him, the rascal of the county.

Her gesture got him straight through the heart. He almost held his hand up to it, because it was as if she hadn't needed to put that hole in him before seeing through him.

Silence wedged between them as he kept right on aching. And it wasn't just in his nethers, either. He was dying to touch her hair. Dying to see what she would do if he just reached out to her, stroking a finger over her cheek, her collarbone.

Damned hormones. Damned blood still pounding through him, driving him to distraction and agony.

"Will you tell me one thing?" he asked, unable to help himself.

"Depends on the question."

"How much of a dream *was* it?"

She pulled those covers around her even tighter.

"Nicki?" he asked softly.

During her hesitation, he found his answer: at some point, even if she'd been sleeping when he'd come in, she'd known what was going on—that it'd been real.

And she'd let it continue.

She stood from the bed. "You really should go."

An inexplicable urge captured him—a draw that he'd never encountered before. Was it because she was the one woman who didn't seem to want him?

All his life, he'd chased and chased, even while running from Pine Junction. Chasing had been the one thing that had occupied him, entertained him.

But this wasn't a mere game. Nicki had been a good girl, and he always drew the line at those, because good girls were trouble.

So why was he still here?

"That outlaw thing did something for you," he said.

From the way she whipped her gaze over to him, he knew that his aim had been true.

"You don't need to worry about it," she said, "because it's never going to happen again."

"You sure about that?" Shane asked. "Because I'd venture to say that you were pretty enthusiastic this time."

Nicki stared at him, her gaze wide.

"What other fantasies do you have, Nicki?" he asked, just daring her to tell him.

NICKI HELD HER BREATH.

Other fantasies.

She thought of her favorites—vampires in moody foreign castles, storm-tossed shipwreck islands and faraway desert tents. All fake, all so appealing, anyway.

She wouldn't dare confess any of it, though.

But looking at Shane now, with his chiseled features, deep blue eyes and imposing frame garbed in black, she longed for…more. She yearned to be taken to another world, to have his hands and mouth all over her, as if she were the only person who drove him to the intensity she'd experienced in him tonight.

"That's none of your business," she said.

Nicki didn't have the heart to utter the rest: *Were you here for just the sex or because you thought you'd be having sex with* me…?

As he stood there, he looked just as needful as she felt, his gaze a little hazy as he kept watching her.

Her pulse jerked, and she loosened her grip on the covers.

It was as if she was in that outlaw dream/fantasy again—a place where she'd had no responsibility, where she wasn't the Nicki who had so much going on in reality.

But she'd been nothing more than a mistake tonight,

and even if he wanted to talk about fantasies now, she wouldn't give in.

Nicki pointed toward her door.

He paused, and she wondered what was going through his mind, especially since he seemed…

Was "rejected" the right word?

He—Shane Carter—the one all the women had gathered round tonight at the party?

Before she could absorb that, he fixed his hat back on his head, nodding to her. When he grinned, it was as if he was trying to show that it didn't matter, but it struck her as wrong.

"Again," he said, "sorry about the trouble." He paused. "And, if it makes any difference, I'm glad it happened. Real glad."

Glad?

With that piece of news, she watched him go through her door, then shut it behind him. Her pulse fluttered like a dying thing as she sat on her bed, her brain finally catching up to everything that'd just happened.

Shane Carter, asking her about her fantasies, seeming as if he would make more than a few of them come true for her.

Shane Carter, glad that he'd been fooled into being here, in this bed…

Downstairs, she thought she heard the door close.

As her skin kept tingling, Nicki lay down on the mattress. And, even though she knew he'd gone, she kept listening for any footfalls outside her door, wishing she would hear the outlaw coming to his hideaway just one more time before the sun rose.

4

What other fantasies do you have...?

After a round of chores the next morning, Nicki sat on the back porch swing near the kitchen exit, fixing the seam on a Halloween princess costume for one of the ranch kids.

She couldn't forget what Shane had said to her.

What he'd *done* to her.

She blew out a breath as a zing of remembrance flew through her, playing electric havoc in her belly, then tingling lower. Just the thought of him made her shift a little on the swing, sending it to creaking.

It was an addiction, running last night over and over again in her mind, reconstructing what it'd been like to feel his mouth near her neck, his hot breath in her ear.

Not a word...

The porch screen door slammed open and three kids spilled out, giggling and waving at Nicki as they ran past, rousing a couple of Australian shepherd ranch dogs who'd been poking around an old oak tree.

"Hi, Nic!" they called out.

"Hey," she said, straightening up and pushing all thoughts of last night away. "What's the ruckus about?"

"We saw Candace in her lady nightie!" Giggle, giggle.

As the lot of them scrambled toward the employee cabins where they lived, Nicki laughed and refocused on the princess costume. Her face was burning in a blush and she hoped no one would see it.

When Candace came out of the door, too, Nicki stiffened. She'd been dreading this moment. She'd avoided talking to her last night, not knowing if she should be angry at Candace or give her a big old hug for...

Well, for procuring Shane like any old-time cathouse lady would've.

Nicki's first instinct was to sink down in that porch swing. Procuring. It sounded real tawdry.

But... *Tawdry.*

The sound of it was adventurous—something Nicki had never been in her life. Except for last night.

A need swelled in her, something just short of a drug she wanted with every hopping molecule in her body.

Candace stepped outside in her short, silky "lady nightie" kimono, yawning, stretching up and smiling at the rising sun.

Then she saw Nicki sitting there, and her expression went cautious as she moved toward the swing.

"Morning."

Nicki had been planning what to say for hours, as she'd lain there in bed, a sexual insomniac.

Mad. She was supposed to be mad at Candace, who was waiting there with bated breath, as if she wanted good news about Nicki's tryst so badly.

Candace said, "I didn't know if I should knock on your door this morning or stay away."

Something perverse in Nicki wanted Candace to squirm a little.

"Didn't you have company?" Candace added.

"Not this morning."

Candace looked as if she was about to explode either with questions or remorse now.

"Okay, okay," Nicki said. "You know darn well what happened last night."

Candace sat on the swing, sending it back then forward ever so slightly. Her bedhead hair was in raucous, red disarray. "And...?"

"You wrote that note."

A cautious nod. "Yes, I did."

"I should strangle you."

"You should?"

"I can't believe you did it."

"I'm sorry, Nic. I just wanted to give you a... Well, a little push. Otherwise you'd go right back to that office and hiding away." She plucked at her kimono. "Did the note work?"

"Yes, the outlaw did come into my room. *While I was sleeping.*"

"Sleeping?"

"That's right."

Now Candace looked more remorseful. "But you woke up."

"Eventually."

It seemed as if Candace was mentally going over what she'd written in that note, and she sucked in a breath, as if understanding that Shane had probably started seducing a slumbering Nicki because it'd been suggested that he should.

Nicki held Candace over the fire a little longer, stitching up the costume in her lap.

"I thought you'd be awake," Candace said. "That's what you said in your phone message, and I thought that when you saw him in your doorway, you'd be flattered. That maybe you'd even throw caution to the wind and go for it."

And Nicki sure had. But, oddly enough, there was no regret on her part, just a craving for more from a man who was clearly damned good at what he did in any bedroom.

A pointed yearning spun through Nicki: images of all her dreams coming true, just for as long as Shane would be here in town. Goose bumps from the longing to be whatever she wanted with him.

"*Did* you go for it after you woke up?" asked Candace.

Nicki just smiled again.

"You!" Candace laughed, clearly relieved. "And here I thought you were going to strangle me."

"I rethought that."

"So…" Candace leaned forward. "Are you going to tell me about it?"

"Nope."

Candace leaned back in the swing. The wind toyed with stray wisps of hair. "It doesn't matter. I don't need every detail—I'm just glad to see you happy. That was the purpose, anyway."

Nicki put down the costume, rested her hand on Candace's shoulder. Her cousin had only done something daring to try and improve Nicki's life. And it could even work again if Nicki dropped her pride and accepted Shane's implied offer of trying out another fantasy....

"Just one thing?" Candace asked, as if there were a million more questions coming, even after this.

"What?"

"Will there be another time, with Shane? Or was he a passing thing?"

Nicki didn't answer, because she was *this* close to blurting that Shane wasn't just a passing anything.

He was...

What? Good heavens, everyone knew that he wasn't a long-term kind of guy. It was just that he'd made her feel so...well, special in a way, unlike anyone had made her feel before. Alive to the world. Even now her skin was still buzzing from him.

But it'd only been sexual. Foreplay. A teasing game.

A something she *could* have again, if she wanted it badly enough.

Candace must've seen the want of it written all over Nicki—it was obvious from the glow in Candace's eyes, that naughty matchmaker's addiction.

"If he's not a passing thing," her cousin said, "*you* should write a note next time."

Nicki saw that Candace's happiness for her was genuine. It was catching, too, and she started to wonder why she *wouldn't* take Shane up on his offer.

He was Shane Carter, everything she'd always wanted, and all she had to do was say yes.

Nicki realized that she'd already come to her senses and changed her mind from last night.

"Next time," she said, "I think I'll just ask him in person."

Just as Candace was about say more, the ranch kids came running by. They'd obviously gotten tired of whatever amusements they'd found in the cabins, and they were messing around in back of the main house now.

Candace demurely tucked her hands under her legs, tucked away all talk of sex and good times. Instead, she nodded at the cowgirl garb Nicki was wearing: her newest pair of jeans, weathered boots, a checkered shirt tied at her waist. Even so, Nicki could tell she was beside herself with excitement about Shane.

"Is this what you're wearing for today's meeting?"

Business talk. Good call.

Nicki touched one of her braids. "I was going for the cowgirl look. I mean, when the investment guy comes out here, he'll want something genuine."

But Candace wasn't swayed. Brassy as ever, she began to unbraid Nicki's hair.

Another makeover?

"Hey," Nicki said, protecting her no-fuss do.

"You look like you're a refugee from the *Dukes of Hazzard*—and not in a good Daisy kind of way." Candace got one of the braids undone. "Now, there we go."

Nicki remembered last night, how Shane had touched her hair, how he'd seemed to like it, even though, most days, it was all she could do to tame it.

But why tame anything now?

As Candace took care of the other braid, then got up from the swing to go inside, Nicki looked in the direction of the Slanted C, toward Shane.

Toward what she could have again if she would only take that next wonderfully tawdry step.

OVER AT THE Slanted C Ranch, Shane was hammering away at a plank in a barn that had been left for useless in favor of a second, fancier one. His brother, Tommy, had never been much for fixing and building on what they already had. Shiny and new—that'd always been Tommy's preference.

This particular plank was a replacement for one of many that had suffered from rot during the ensuing years, just like a lot of things around this place.

After a particularly energetic slam, a voice sounded from behind Shane.

"Frustrated?"

The rusty-hinge tone belonged to Walter, a shaggy-gray-haired, bow-legged hell-of-a-horse-breeding man who'd been in charge of operations at the Slanted C ever since Shane was a kid. He'd stayed on after Shane had moved north of Dallas, away from his father and toward his future on a smaller spread. Walter had even been here after Barry Carter's death, when Tommy had taken over.

And that's when the rot had gone to a whole new level, Shane thought as he slid his hammer into his tool belt, then lifted his hat, wiping a slick of sweat from his brow.

"What makes you think I'm taking my ire out on a poor piece of wood?" Shane asked.

Walter handed him a bottle of water, and Shane drank it up. The older man didn't even bother to answer Shane's rhetorical question.

"A load of things eating away underneath, ain't there?" Walter said instead.

He meant the ranch, but he could've just as well been talking about Shane.

Walking out of the barn, he pulled his hat lower, taking in the hay-laced morning air, the spread of grass in front of him, leading to paddocks over the hill and the new barn. Over another hill, the Square W+W Ranch waited, too.

So did Nicki, and when Shane wasn't hammering at something, he remembered how she'd taken him away from the rot last night, making him feel like a new man for a short while.

And he wasn't just talking about being in the role of an outlaw. He'd forgotten just about everything while he was with Nicki, and he couldn't explain why or how.

He looked toward the north fence line, recalling a day when Nicki had fallen from a broken rail. His dad had already been tearing into her when Shane had ridden ahead, not thinking about anything other than if she was hurt or what might happen if Barry Carter got to her before Shane did.

When he'd seen that she was all right, he'd immediately shielded her from his dad, but by that time, the old man had gotten hold of himself, donning that cover that only his family fully saw beneath. Still, when he'd turned his horse around, he'd sent Shane a look that indicated there'd be hell to pay back home for even hinting to anyone outside the family that Barry Carter was someone else entirely.

When Shane had looked down at Nicki again, the gratefulness—maybe even the awe—on her face had taken him to another place for a moment. It had shown him that he could matter, even in some little way, to someone else.

But he didn't know why he was thinking of Nicki now, when she'd told him she wouldn't see him again.

Walter had followed him outside, crossing his arms over his striped shirt. "I hear the W+W is hosting a picnic for that businessman today. You going there?"

"I wasn't planning on it."

"I don't blame you. Your dad would be turning over in his grave to know that Nicki is even thinking about welcoming dudes. Can you just imagine what kind of blue words would fly out of his mouth at that?"

Shane didn't want to imagine, because with those so-called "blue words," there'd always been more, and they'd left bruises.

Are you stupid, drag racing on the back roads, boy?

Why can't you just smarten up like your brother?

See if I can't knock some sense into your head with this—

Shane steeled himself from the memory of his dad's fist coming at him, then began to walk away. "In Nicki Wade's defense, she's only trying to make sure everyone on that ranch has a job, come the end of the year."

The old man strolled next to Shane, giving him a surprised glance, his bushy eyebrows arched. "Listen to you."

Even Walter couldn't have had a grasp of just how far Tommy had run the Slanted C into the ground. He also didn't know that when Russell Alexander had called Shane, just to inquire if he was interested in turning the Slanted C into a dude resort with him staying on as a consultant, that there'd been a moment of temptation.

But he would find another way to get back in the flush. There had to be one, and it'd be a way that wouldn't involve public knowledge of the Carter family's woes.

Shane would make it all right, even if the perfect son, Tommy, hadn't. It'd always been that way, whether it was Tommy crashing the family pickup and Shane covering for him in a moment of pity, or Tommy taking the Carter family's savings and saying he would double them, only to wipe them out.

"My main concern," Shane said, "is that a shark like Russell Alexander doesn't take Nicki Wade for all she's worth. Businessmen like him know how to wheel-and-deal, and from what I hear, Nicki is desperate to save her place."

"So you *are* going over there, then?"

Shane stopped walking.

"I mean," Walter said, "you're gonna do what her daddy and mama would've expected a neighbor to do and watch over her?"

"She's an adult, Walter."

At the thought of last night, something went off-kilter in his chest. She'd told him there wouldn't be more encounters between them, but from the look in her eyes, he'd wondered.

He drank the last of his water, looking toward the W+W. Yup, he'd wondered.

"Maybe I'll go on over there later," he said, "just to see what's what."

Just to see that Nicki didn't fall into the clutches of a true bad guy.

THE WEATHER COULDN'T HAVE been better for a picnic on this Saturday, and the sun shone down over the hay bales that everyone on the W+W had set out near an abandoned, plank-withered, paint-stripped barn. Children climbed over the stacks, playing tag and hide-and-seek, using ropes to try to lasso the fake pony heads that were attached to some of the bales.

There were also gingham cloth-covered tables holding a bevy of country food that Nicki had splurged on— beans that had been cooked over the fire that crackled in the middle of the festivities, carne asada plus all the trimmings for soft tacos, ribs and corn on the cob. A wagon was rolling around, too, driven by Manny, transporting the ranch kids back and forth from the regular stables, where they were taking out the horses today for rides.

Among it all, the representative from the Lyon Group stood, and Nicki surveyed the man she would need to impress in order to perhaps partner with his business and use his money to keep the ranch alive, all while keeping on her crew, too.

Maybe.

Russell Alexander, who looked to be in his early thirties, was dressed in what Candace had told Nicki was a Versace suit, as cool as Cary Grant, even in the mild heat. Tall and broad-shouldered, he had his black hair slicked back in a hundred-dollar-plus haircut, if Nicki were to guess.

Altogether, Alexander possessed a sixties smoothness about him—a man with a certain throwback gloss and masculinity that made him even more imposing.

Candace sidled up next to Nicki. "He was nice enough when you greeted him. He seemed absolutely charmed."

"I think he's the type who always seems charmed, just so he doesn't have to tell you what he's really thinking." Nicki looked at him sidelong. "There's something about him that's hard to grasp."

As he bent down to Kirby, the four-year-old tow-headed son of one of the ranch hands, Mr. Alexander offered the child a cupcake.

"Yes," Candace said. "He's definitely suspicious. Just look at him operate—you can't put any faith in a man who's nice to children."

"You're hilarious, Candy." Nicki smoothed down her white blouse. It was sleeveless, chic and straight from Candace's closet. Candace had paired it with the only nice pants Nicki owned—a pair of tan trousers that Candace had ironed until the things practically stood up themselves.

Nicki had insisted on wearing her Sunday pair of hand-worked, tooled leather boots, though.

Candace squeezed her bare arm. "You're sure this is what you want to do with the ranch?"

Nicki sighed. "It's either this or start letting some of the staff go."

"I could make more calls to my old professors and classmates from business school. Maybe they, or my friends, have come up with ideas for us by now."

"Keep doing that, Candy. Meanwhile…" Nicki nodded toward Russell Alexander.

"I'd wish you luck if I thought you needed it," Candace said.

"Thanks. But there's one thing I might need instead of luck."

"What's that?"

"You." Nicki gave one glance to Candace's blossoming yellow sundress, with its halter that gave modest shelter to her buxomness. She'd worn her red hair straight today, and it shimmied down her back.

"If you see that I don't have Russell Alexander interested," Nicki said, "you have my blessing to swoop in and help me out."

"Me?"

"You're the businesswoman."

Candace got serious. "Anything you ask. I'll be keeping my eye out for any SOS signs."

Nicki was sure she would, and she set out to win over Mr. Alexander, breathing in, out, her nerves jangling just under her skin.

Aside from the Slanted C next door, which boasted a small lake, Nicki knew she had the most beautiful, versatile ranch in the area, with a shady creek running through it and the best horseflesh in the county, although hard times had cut down on the size of what they had to offer. So, as she made her way to Russell Alexander, her stride grew even more confident.

Now he was at the hors d'oeuvres table, filling a plate with bacon-wrapped chestnuts. He grinned at the food, as if it was country-time *charming.*

When Nicki approached him, he glanced at her, and she could've sworn he'd already dismissed her in the first eighth of a second.

Had he already made up his mind about where he'd be investing his firm's money before she could even sell him on the W+W?

Think again, Mr. Alexander.

"How's the grub?" she asked.

"Hearty and appealing," he said in an offhanded way that wouldn't be so out of place in an old movie, either. "It'd bring back memories of my summer camp days if I had any."

Right, she thought. This man had probably started

interning at Fortune 500 companies when he was six, leaving his summers full.

She gestured toward the child-and-hay-choked wagon, which was ready to get underway on another trip to the stables. "I'd love to show you our horses, take you on a tour when you're ready."

He glanced down at his suit.

"Or," she said, realizing he wasn't really dressed for a ride, "maybe we could save the activities for another day?"

"Maybe that could be arranged."

Was there a ring of reluctance in his tone? Had he come here just to appease her?

Again, she wondered if he'd already set his sights on another location, and her determination doubled.

"You came to Pine Junction at a good time," she said. "During sunny days like these, we fish, ride and hike on my ranch. We've got the renovated barn, too, so we've got rainy days covered. It's like a community hub where you could do crafts, activities, have dances...."

"Ideal."

But, by now, he wasn't looking at Nicki anymore.

Nope—his eyes were trained on something just behind her.

A smile stretched across Russell Alexander's face— the kind of smile a man got when he was *truly* interested in something.

Or someone.

Candace joined them, all sunny and bright in her flowy dress. "The guest of honor," she said a bit breathlessly.

"The honor's mine," he said, extending his hand for a shake, balancing his plate in his other hand.

Their grips lingered, and with one subtle look to Nicki, Candace let her know that she'd seen how a little extra "oomph" was required.

"I'm Nicki's assistant," Candace said. "It'll be my job to show you around, if you have the time."

Nicki smiled at the man just before Candace started to lead him toward a table so he could eat. All the while, she talked about the ranch and what she loved about it.

Impressed, Nicki let her teammate take over, knowing Candace would deliver a much-improved investment businessman back to her.

One who'd probably even be that much nearer to discussing a deal that would save her from dismantling the ranch piece by piece.

CANDACE WAS MAKING great headway—and, in spite of her best intentions, it wasn't just of the business sort, either.

The moment she'd seen Russell Alexander step foot onto the ranch, her inner radar had started to beep in a spot that tingled inside her.

She liked how he carried himself. It reminded her of success, of the city, and she'd sorely missed both, even if she loved being out here with Nicki.

When, from across the way, she'd seen how Russell Alexander slightly tilted his body from Nicki while she'd made her pitch about the ranch, Candace had understood pronto that an opportunity was slipping away from the W+W, and fast.

She wouldn't blow this opportunity. No, sir. But, little by little, as she small-talked with Russell Alexander, Candace realized that there was more than just ranch talk afoot right now.

He was enjoying her.

Maybe that could be a good thing, if she could steer that energy in the right direction.

She knew men like him; she'd dated some businessmen and spent a lot of time in high-reaching social circles at San Diego charity auctions and dinners with fellow graduates from her college business program. Sometimes she suspected that their interest in her was mainly due to the way in which she put visiting clients and prospective networking contacts at ease.

But, hey, if schmoozing and putting people at ease was her sole talent in life, she wasn't complaining.

"So," she said, resting her chin in her hand as she leaned her elbow on the table and he ate, "what have you been doing to have fun in Pine Junction?"

"I haven't been here long enough to do much." He had a way of talking... Confident but not arrogant. Somehow, he was a gentleman with a rough edge that lay more under his skin than on it.

Interesting.

"There's plenty to do here," she said, smiling.

As if wanting to cool herself, she raised a bottle of soda pop that she'd plucked from a bucket of ice at the end of the table. She placed it against her chest, right above the rise of her breasts.

She hadn't meant it to be a come-on, but somehow, most things she did ended up that way. And when Russell Alexander's deep gray eyes rested on that bottle, then rose to meet her gaze again, he was giving her that look she'd seen a thousand times before.

You coming on to me?

Shoot. She was here to sell the ranch, not herself.

His smile barely brushed his lips, and she knew exactly what he was thinking.

The girls at the Square W+W were using every trick in the book.

Double shoot. Candace casually took a drink of soda, shrugging, then said, "Maybe I should just let you eat, Mr. Alexander."

"Russell," he said.

"Russell." That was a positive sign, showing he was still receptive. "If I'm nattering away too much, just let me know. We're only excited about the possibilities here."

"Possibilities."

Okay. *He* wasn't talking about business, was he?

It was just in the way he said it.

"Unless I'm wrong," she said, "your company wants to invest in a property. It's no secret."

"You heard it through the grapevine?"

"Just one of the advantages of living in a small town."

"Yes…one of them." He smiled again—the barest of bare smiles.

He was making her wonder yet again.

Her pulse beat in her throat, adrenaline pumping. She'd left the city, but it seemed as if it'd come to her in the form of this man, and she felt as if a million lights had lit through her, making her glow like a skyline.

But…business before pleasure. She couldn't mess this up for Nicki, and all the rest of the residents who depended on the ranch. Now that she thought about it, that included her for the time being.

"Okay then…" she said. "How would later today or tomorrow be for a horseback ride?"

He extracted an iPhone from an inside jacket pocket. With every movement, he made a vein in her neck pulsate. All she had to do was get a glimpse of his hands, with their blunt fingers. She could imagine how they'd feel running over her, skin on skin, tracing her stomach, then parting her legs...

Candace shifted, her clit stiff, just from the brief fantasy. She'd been like a nun out here in the country, mostly because she liked her guys cosmopolitan. She also hadn't wanted to embarrass Nicki by being the "wild city cousin" and taking any man who caught her fancy to bed, even though, in her natural vivaciousness, she talked about it nonstop.

As she waited for Russell to finish checking his schedule, she glanced around for Nicki, who was talking with Cook at the barbecue area, sending a furtive glance at Candace every once in a while.

Candace gave her a sly thumbs-up and returned her attention to Russell.

He punched something into his phone, then peered up, watching her with a look that made her temperature rise, flames licking at her belly until desire melted down and coated her sex.

He spoke. "I've got teleconferences the rest of the day as well as...meetings. Other than that..."

The remainder of it hung there, ready for the taking.

"What would you think about a morning tour?" she asked carefully. "Tomorrow? Ten-thirty, say? Brunch afterward?"

He nodded, inputting the time into his phone. "Let's skip the horseback ride, though. I've been getting plenty of those."

It was an outright reference to how he was checking out other locales for a dude resort.

Ruffled by that, she said, "Noted. But you'd better come *here* hungry."

His fingers hovered above the phone screen, as if her words had the effect of her physically skimming her fingers over him—inappropriate, surprising, sultry. The lust flared in her again. But then he finished inputting and slid the phone back into his inner jacket pocket.

"Tomorrow, then," he said, standing, grinning at her as if he appreciated everything she'd brought to the table.

It was only when he was gone that she started to second-guess herself.

Had she just gotten into a compromising situation? Had she somehow promised more than just a ranch tour?

She watched Russell go over to Nicki, who was standing by the dessert table. He shook her hand, then walked toward the house, where he'd parked his black Mercedes.

After he was gone, Candace sent Nicki a more emphatic, slightly hopeful, thumbs-up. Nicki's answering smile made everything all right.

Candace rose from the table, intending to go over and give the total lowdown, but she stopped in her tracks as someone else approached her cousin.

And when Nicki, herself, turned around and saw Shane Carter, as if she had felt him even before he had arrived, Candace immediately changed direction and walked the opposite way.

She couldn't help a huge smile. It seemed she had already closed one deal and, with any luck, her streak was only going to continue with Russell Alexander.

5

"HI, NICKI."

Shane waited for her to turn around, and every second until she did slowed down like a drawn-out heartbeat inside of him.

He didn't expect the crash of his blood when she met his gaze, the brutal, breaking wave of lust that beat in his chest, then whirled down to his gut. Even in a simple blouse that revealed her toned, tanned arms, plus the modest pants that hugged her long legs, she was enough to turn him on just as powerfully as she'd done last night in a corset and fishnet stockings.

She pushed back a hank of curly hair from her face, which was flushed either from the sun or…

The memory of last night?

If she was embarrassed about it, she recovered quickly enough, returning to the feisty woman at the Halloween party who'd given him as good as she'd gotten when he'd confronted her about duding out her ranch.

"Are you just here to put a heroic halt to all the evil change that's overtaking Pine Junction?" she asked.

He propped his booted foot on a picnic bench, resting his arm on his thigh and tipping back his hat. "I was thinking about doing just that, but it appears the forces of evil have already vacated the premises."

Glancing in the direction of where the suit—the tall man who'd stood out like a sore thumb—had disappeared, Shane didn't say anything to Nicki about how Russell Alexander had tried to get a show-me-the-ranch appointment out of him, too.

But he did say, "You know that this Alexander guy is taking a look-see at other properties this afternoon, right?"

"Yes, I do."

They went silent, and suddenly it wasn't about dude resorts anymore. It was about what they'd done…what he'd said at the end of last night—a question Nicki hadn't quite answered when he'd asked if she had any more fantasies.

A gaggle of children were chasing one another nearby, laughing and using squirt guns by the entrance to the old barn. Adult employees had relaxed now that the businessman had left, and some of them had even joined the kids in their games.

Shane kept his voice low. "About last night…"

"Yes," she said, interrupting him, meeting his gaze head-on with her own.

She'd taken Shane off guard.

Yes, she'd said.

But yes to what?

His body already knew, and it was warming up, just like the low grumble of an engine in a car that was used to going fast, not driving slow.

Nicki crossed her arms over her chest as she continued, keeping her volume low, too. "Yes," she said again.

"Yes?" he asked.

She looked at him as if he was a devil, and maybe he was—or, at least, he had a wicked talent for getting under her skin.

"Well," she said, "I figure there's no reason to be mad at you for last night. Candace and I straightened it all out. And I also figure that it's high time I got out more...."

And he just kept on with the devilry, his skin on fire for her. "I'm still not sure what you're trying to tell me."

She huffed out a sigh. "For a man with all your experience, you sure aren't connecting the dots very well."

"Maybe I just want to hear you say what you have to say."

"And what would that be? That you might not be in town all that long and we should—"

"I won't be." Not if he could help it. He didn't want to spend more time than he needed to on that ranch.

He wanted to hear her say it.

"Do you want me to tell you that I had fun last night and I wouldn't mind having some more?" she asked, braver now.

But her gaze was wide again, as if even she couldn't believe that she was admitting to wanting another night with him.

"I want you to say all of it, Nicki."

She was blushing again, and this time he knew that it wasn't because she'd been under too much Indian summer sun.

He had some power over her, didn't he? And God help him, but he liked the sense of that. In a life where he'd had precious little of it with all the problems that had befallen the Carters and all the responsibility that had fallen on him, warranted or not, he liked it.

He leaned forward, closer to her—close enough to smell the spring shampoo in all those curls he was dying to touch.

"Are you asking for your outlaw to come back to you tonight?" he said.

As she hesitated, her breathing suddenly uneven, he wondered if she wanted to lean over, sink against him, just as much as he wanted her to do it.

Then she burned him with that direct, light green gaze. "That's what I'm asking. For…him…to come back."

He wanted to reach out, run a finger over her arm, both of which had loosened away from her chest as she peered at him, in on the joke by now, obviously willing to tease him back. The quirk of her mouth even poked him in the heart ever so slightly.

But this wasn't about hearts. It was about sex, giving a jump start to both her and him, then getting out of her bedroom before he stayed too long.

"If that outlaw of yours were to come back," he said, "where would he meet you this time?"

She slid a glance toward the barn, then looked away as one of the kids broke away from the water fight and sprinted past them.

They stayed quiet until the child darted back to the action.

"Midnight," she said. "That's when I'll be here."

He didn't say anything more, but he did take the risk on subtly running his knuckle over her arm as he walked away, watching as goose bumps rose over her skin.

She slowly drew away, then grabbed a dessert plate,

as if suspecting that everyone was watching them. But when Shane looked around, they didn't have anyone's attention.

Her message was clear, though. This was to be a private assignation—a fling only for quiet, keep-to-herself Nicki Wade and him to know about while hiding the truth from everyone else.

Had she ever done something like this before?

It made him wonder just how well he actually did know his neighbor.

It, by God, even intrigued him.

He grabbed a plate, too, moseying over to the barbecue, already pretending he was disinterested in Nicki.

Pretending that he was something that he really wasn't in everyone else's eyes but hers.

WHEN NICKI FINALLY LEFT the picnic, she went straight to the main house, where Zeke, one of her cowboys, had said he'd seen Candace heading earlier.

Indeed, she found her in her bedroom, sitting at an old cream-and-gold vanity table Candace had found at a yard sale last weekend. She'd discovered an old-fashioned ice-cream-parlor-type wire chair to go along with it, as well as a long, fog-traced mirror that she'd propped against a wall near her red-quilted bed. She'd purchased some sheer deep pink material from the fabric store to drape over the top of the mirror, and also bought a big Betty Grable poster to lord it over a corner of the room, giving the place some flair.

Somehow, in the short time Candace had been here, she'd decorated her domain with a far more invested hand than Nicki ever had done to her own room. But Nicki had never paid much mind to that kind of thing—

she'd always been more focused on stuff like feeding the horses, blanketing and turning them out, cleaning the stalls, mixing the grain, working the stock... All that, plus learning how to balance account books that never seemed to find their equilibrium.

In the mirror above the vanity table, Candace saw Nicki standing in her doorway, and she turned around on that wire ice cream chair.

"Tell me you've got a date tonight."

Nicki blinked. Was she that readable?

Candace laughed, leaning on the back of the chair. "I saw Shane walking over to you at the picnic."

"And I saw you getting along with Russell Alexander."

"He's...an interesting man. And he put me on his calendar for a meeting tomorrow morning. I'm going to show him around the ranch."

"Seriously?"

"Seriously."

Candace faced the mirror again, and Nicki would've said her cousin looked smug except for the delighted, adorable way in which she plucked a tube of lipstick from her makeup tray, then used it to test the shimmery pink color on her lips.

"You did it, then," Nicki said. "You reeled him in."

Candace paused in applying the makeup. "Yes, I did."

But the hint of regret—about the ranch going dude—was too much, and Nicki put the thought of seeing the W+W change so drastically aside.

"It looks to me like you've got those lipsticks lined up like bullets," she said. "Is that going to be how you handle Mr. Alexander?"

"Russell." Candace smacked her lips, considering the color on them in the mirror. "And better bullets than bras with him."

"What do you mean?"

"I'm approaching this as I'd approach a job. They didn't call me the Enforcer for nothing at my desk. I had my executive's life in precision order."

Candace was puckering her lips now, seeming just about as innocent as Rita Hayworth in a red dress. Nicki had no doubt she was the most efficient enforcer in history.

Nicki cocked her head. "I'm getting a vibe about your 'interest' in 'Russell.'"

Candace snapped the lipstick back in its tube. "Okay. I admit that there's something about him."

Sitting down on the bed, Nicki thought about the businessman. Sure, she could see how someone so dapper might appeal to a city girl like Candace. Russell Alexander was suave, nicely put together. He looked as if he might smell of cocktail hour bourbon and money.

"I'm not surprised," she said, "that a classy guy like him would get to you."

"It's not the 'classy' thing." Candace crossed one shapely leg over the other, her yellow sundress belling around her. "There's just something about him that makes me want to rip off that suit and get at what's underneath. Know what I mean?"

Memories of pulling open Shane's shirt last night thrummed through Nicki.

Yes, she knew.

She took a breath, clearing her head. "I can tell you why you're interested—he seems hard to get. You like that in a man. You always have. I remember Josh

Tanner—that cowboy we had on the ranch when we were in high school. He was out of college, but you set your cap for him, anyway…."

"Because he wouldn't look twice at me, even though I caught him doing just that during the spring rodeo in town once. Your point is made."

"But that's what kept you interested in him—that one look." Nicki hoped Alexander hadn't given Candace too many of those. This had to be about business, not, as Candace had said, bras.

"Wouldn't a look do the same for you?" Candace lifted her brow as she deftly changed the subject. "Speaking of getting a look…or copping a feel… *Are* you seeing Shane again?"

Nicki smiled.

"Bra-*vo*." She got out of her chair, came to the bed, started fussing with Nicki's hair.

"What…" Nicki shooed her off. "Again with the hair?"

"We've got to go with another style tonight. Can't bore him with the same old thing."

"I wasn't going to. I mean…" Nicki bit her lip.

"Tell me," Candace said. "Come on."

Nicki hadn't said anything to Shane about it, but she had something else in mind for tonight. And why not? She had a lot of time to make up for.

"I'm all for the outlaw games," she said. "But… He asked me last night what other fantasies I had. And I started thinking…"

Candace gave her that "And…?" look.

"Well, I started thinking that I can have *anything* with him." Her gaze went a little bleary with sensual greed. She couldn't remember any other time when there hadn't been any constraints on her.

And now, the world—and Shane—was her oyster.

How many people in life would pass judgment on what got her going? Shane didn't. Actually, he seemed up for anything, and all that had been stopping Nicki before was herself.

Nicki's gaze brushed over the room's second-hand furniture, beaten wooden floors and carpets that needed replacing…

She hadn't had it all in life, but now she had the chance to be rich if she wanted to, just like one of the strong women who controlled hearts and destinies in her books. She had the opportunity to be as sinful, wealthy or decadent as she pleased, even for a night.

Candace stood, going to her closet, where a burst of colorful clothing waited. She started to go through the offerings.

"Since you can have anything," she said, "what's it going to be? A Hollywood star from the forties who plucks a gorgeous fan from out of the crowd? A prim, proper heiress who seduces the chauffeur? We can go to the city before your rendezvous time to get whatever you need if I don't have it here."

But Nicki already knew what she wanted—and she doubted even Candace would have all she needed in that closet of hers.

NICKI AND CANDACE had returned from a trip to the city just after eight o'clock. It allowed Nicki enough time to shower, then give herself over to the cosmetically awesome talents of Candace.

By midnight, Nicki was all dressed up with some-one to do.

Now, as she sat on an old milking stool in the aban-doned barn, which had been kept clean and tidy enough for the kids to play games in it by day, she smoothed her flowy, ankle-length crimson skirt over her lap. They'd found it at the Goodwill store in the city, along with a nearly sheer, tight, sexy peasant-type top that laced up the front. At a costume store, which had been filled with customers for Halloween, they'd discovered a half-corset, and it was making Nicki's breath come short.

She was also wearing stockings—Candace had sug-gested that she rip them to go along with the fantasy's scenario—and Nicki's otherwise bare feet rested on one of the blankets she'd laid out on the dirt, along with some white picnic blankets she'd used to cover some hay bales, which were supposed to be makeshift beds. Above her, she'd hung a couple of lanterns, too, hoping they would add to the illusion that this might be another place, another time.

A pirate ship in need of a pirate.

She glanced at her outdated cell phone—11:56—then tucked it behind a bale, out of sight, out of modern mind.

Then she heard a sound outside. Someone moving. Someone coming in.

She saw him in the doorway—Shane in his hat, his cowboy outlaw gear shadowed by moonlight. Shane, rogue and reluctant good guy…

She lay down on a makeshift bed, spreading her un-bound hair over a pillow.

Tingles whirred up and down her body, settling to a

vibrating gnaw between her legs. She already felt ready, plumped and damp.

Shane stepped into the barn, drawing the door closed behind him. It was dim where he was standing, and that dimness allowed her some courage that she'd only had in business, not romance, before now.

"Take off the hat," she said. "Then the bandanna. There are some things by the door for you."

He laughed, low and oh-so-manly. "Looks like you're awake tonight."

"Tonight's different. For one thing, you're not the same outlaw." And, tonight, she really *was* awake, in more ways than one.

"What's going on, Nicki?"

She shifted on the bed, stretching out on her side, letting her skirt ride up one stocking-torn leg. "Next time you look at me, you'll think of how I'm sleeping peacefully. You're going to see a woman you brought here against her will and she's exhausted. But that's not going to stop you."

He didn't move, but she went on, undeterred.

More excited than ever.

"You've just walked into your cabin to find her… me…in your quarters," she whispered now. "I'm the spoils of your ship's attack on a town off the Spanish Main."

As she half-closed her eyelids, she saw him take off the cowboy hat, the bandanna. He spied what she'd left for him near the door, heard him laugh to himself.

She squeezed her legs together because the pierce of need in her clit was pure agony. Just *watching* him was agony because she knew what was coming, anticipated it until she wanted to scream.

No remorse, she thought, no regrets. Not about anything anymore. Tonight was what it was, and she would finally have everything she wanted from him.

Everything…

Untucking the shirt from his pants, he said, "You really think I'm the eye patch type?"

"There's no eye patch there."

"But there's this." He held up a red sash, then a fake rapier.

She "sleepily" rolled to her back, arms above her head. With no bra, her breasts would be outlined against her blouse, her peaked nipples making her desire obvious.

He must've noticed, because she heard him groan softly. Then, from the corner of her gaze, she saw him tie the sash around his waist. But he dropped the rapier to the ground.

As he sauntered over to her, he undid one button on his shirt.

Then another.

"Is this what you had in mind?" he asked.

In response, she dove into the fantasy all the way, sitting up on her pallet, cowering, as if she'd just awakened to see him walk into the cabin—the pirate king she had watched from afar as he'd pillaged and plundered.

Her captor.

"What are you going to do with me?" she asked.

No remorse, no regret…

A side-smile tilted his mouth, his blue eyes sparkling. He was into it.

"I haven't decided just yet…wench."

"My name is—"

"I don't want to know your name."

In one stride, he closed the distance between them, reached out, grasping her ankle, looking mighty entertained by all of this.

"Come off that bed," he said.

She shook her head, her pulse flittery. It was his voice—commanding, gruff. It made her go even wetter.

He pulled her off the pallet, sweeping her to a stand, bringing her flush against his body and making the breath leave her entirely until she somehow got it back. She could feel how stimulated he already was, the bulge in his jeans hard against her belly.

Her breathing sawed through her, and he smiled down at her, as if he'd claimed another victory.

As if she had nowhere to run and he was utterly in control....

But then, as if merely having her in that position had been enough, he let her go, backed away, until he was in the shadows again, this time, much nearer to the pallet.

"You'll do as I say from now on, wench," he said. "Is that clear?"

She shook her head, just as she would've in real life. It was instinctive. No one had ever ordered Nicki around before, and she wasn't sure she liked it now.

Or maybe she did. A lot.

In the dimness, she could barely see him lowering himself to a near-sit, a predator.

"First," he whispered, "you'll take off that damned thing around your waist."

Her corset.

She wasn't about to fight him on this—the thing wasn't comfortable to wear, anyway—so she unlaced it. When it was untied, her breasts lowered from their precipitous height, but she breathed easier, even though it still felt like ice was in her lungs—refreshing, bracing.

After she slid the corset up and over her head, she tossed it his way. In the near darkness, he caught it in mid-air, his hand fisting around it.

"What are you wearing under that skirt?" he asked.

"A woman never tells."

"She will tonight." He gestured with his hand. "You're going to lift it up for me."

This was getting intense, but she did it. In the back of her mind, she almost thought that he might spring out of the shadows at her if she disobeyed, but the fact that she could do so actually empowered her in a way she'd never expected.

She inched up her skirt, and it rustled with every move. When she had revealed her ripped stockings, he spoke again.

"Take those off."

Swallowing, she propped her foot on the pallet. Then, feeling a twinge of ye olde decadence, she bent over, putting her hands on her ankle, sliding her fingers up her silk-covered calf, over her knee, her thigh.

She just about thought she could see the shine of his gaze in the dimness, devouring her.

Then, deliberately, she pushed down the thigh-high stocking, which used some kind of sticky stuff to stay up. Then she repeated the performance with the other.

"Are you done having your way with me?" she whispered, putting some disgust into her voice, the type of superior dismissal she imagined a lady who'd been kidnapped from her beautiful mansion on the cliffs might use with the man who'd taken her away from luxury to…this.

Her pulse quickened.

His tone was gravelly. "Your top. That needs to come off next."

By now, her mouth was dry, her heart kicking, her blood tearing through her.

But she obeyed, anyway, tugging on the lacing that held her blouse together, parting it, allowing the material to rest on her shoulders, offering only a peak of cleavage.

The linen brushed against the tips of her breasts, making her feel so wanton.

Before she knew it, he was on his feet, out of the shadows, taking her in his arms, face to face, mouth near mouth.

But he didn't kiss her.

No—he was fevered, almost even angry for some reason, and he ran a thumb over her lips, tracing the outline.

"I hate what you do to me…." he said.

Driven by his words, she parted her lips, taking his finger into her mouth, sucking on him.

She thought she heard him curse again under his breath, urgently, as she kept sucking, languidly using her tongue now.

For the first time in Nicki's life, she had a man where she wanted him, fantasy or not, and she took his hand from her mouth, guiding it downward so it dragged over her chin, her neck, lower, until he came to her breasts.

Then she let go of him, and he coaxed his fingers over one of her nipples, sending tickles of heat through her, melting, making every part of her liquid.

"Damn," she thought she heard him say again as he cupped her in his palm. He used his thumb to explore, bringing her nipple to a pained, pleasured nub.

She reached up, wanting to feel the features of his face, to touch its contours so she could always have some image in her mind of him, even beyond these games they were playing. Maybe those mental pictures would even last after he left her for good.

But before she could touch him, he leaned her back, using just one of his arms. Then he bent to her, taking her other nipple into his mouth, tonguing, laving, gently biting. It was all Nicki could do to shut up and take it while she arched into him, encouraging him.

So real, she thought. This felt like it was *really* happening, but not like it had after she'd woken up from her dream last night.

This felt as if it could be anything *but* a fantasy.

Turning his attention to her other breast, he worshipped her, making her feel like she was his one, his only, the mere reason he had laid damage to her town tonight—the reason he had lit everything on fire.

To spirit her away.

Only her.

She threaded her fingers through his thick hair, and another stray thought intruded.

Not a pirate.

This was *Shane*.

How many times had she wished for this?

But, long ago, her fantasies had been so much more innocent. And far less…oh…like *this*…

He sucked her breast, kissed the skin between them, then lower, lower, making her squirm.

Then he was coaxing her to her back, easing off her

skirt and tossing it to the floor, leaving her only in her blouse and a pair of drenched undies.

With one practiced move, he parted her legs, and she took in a shaking breath, heard him laugh, as if he knew how excited she was, how close her nerves were to singeing.

His breath came hot and damp against her as he slid her legs over his shoulders.

She was about to whisper his name, but she couldn't say it.

Not tonight.

Maybe not...ever...

When he pressed his mouth against her covered sex, she bit her lower lip, keeping herself from whimpering. But when he started to gnaw through the cotton of her undies, she went and did it anyway, unable to restrain herself.

Her tiny sounds of delight seemed to push him onward, and he went at her harder. Then, as if teasing her wasn't enough for him anymore, he drew aside the crotch of her panties, still keeping them on, and tasted her with his tongue.

She bucked at the needling pleasure in her clit, and he laughed.

"Want more?" he whispered.

In response, she reached for her undies, fumbling with them to get them the hell off.

Torturously, he divested her of the material, tossing it away, too.

Before he bent back down to her, he whispered, "After tonight, I'll..."

"Throw me overboard?"

She'd stepped out of the fantasy with a joke, of all

things, and she knew why. It was because she'd come to want something else from him besides this—she wanted *truth*. Would she always want that from Shane, even though she didn't actually know him and he didn't know her?

He rested his fingertips on her belly, and her muscles clenched, making her feel the maddening tension in her sex, as well. She was so wet for him, and when he edged down, over the curls on her mound, she almost dug her nails into his scalp.

Restless, Nicki did something she'd never dared do in real life—she took control of a man.

She sat up, her breath coming in rasps as she ran her hands up his jeans-clad thighs, and slipped a palm between his legs, nestling his penis, which strained against his jeans.

He grunted, maybe both in surprise and pleasure.

"What're you waiting for?" she whispered, stroking him, teasing him as he'd teased her.

As if having to remind her that he wasn't a man to be trifled with, he reached behind her, threading his hands into her hair, grabbing on.

The slight roughness of his gesture turned her on even more.

Alive...*awake.*

No turning back now, Nicki went for what she wanted the most—a kiss from her childhood crush.

A sign of real affection from the man who'd always had her heart from the very first time he'd been her hero.

6

SOMEWHERE ALONG THE WAY, Shane had lost the upper hand.

It was time to get it back.

As this woman—this fantasy version of a captivated lady—brushed her lips over his, he toyed with her again, drawing away, making her moan in what he thought to be frustration.

This was how it should be—with the guy leading the way. With the pirate, who'd taken her as his, teaching her just where her place was.

Beneath him in bed.

But then she nestled her lips against his throat, kissing him there, sending tiny sparks of want through his groin, making his lips pound.

A kiss. That was obviously what she was asking for.

Shane tightened his hold on her hair, not cruelly, but not quite gently, either.

"None of that," he whispered, near a growl. "Do as I say. Understand?"

She paused, and he took that for agreement.

He tried not to think about how this was his neighbor, Nicki. Tried to stay in the frame of mind that she was his captive, not someone he shouldn't be talking to like this, and that helped.

In this guise, he wouldn't have to explain to her that he didn't go around kissing many women when it came time to bed them. Kissing was the simplest of acts, the first step in a courtship—and that was the issue.

He didn't *court* women, he enjoyed them, just like this pirate would. He pleased them and they pleased him, and, in the end, they sailed off in different directions.

Hell, Shane hadn't even kissed Nicki last night during outlaw time, and that had been no oversight.

Feeling secure in his role again, he raised himself away from her, leaving her on the floor, her skin bare, most of it golden from her time in the sun except for where clothing had covered her.

He ran a slow gaze down her body. Long, lean, her breasts small yet perfect and round, her waist slender, her belly flat, her slim thighs pressed together—a move that wasn't enough to hide the desire that had made the curls between her legs wet.

The sight of her sent daggers through him all over again, weakening him until he untied that ridiculous sash from his hips.

For a second, it seemed that she was experiencing a very real moment as she watched him wrap the sash around both of his hands, then stretch the length of it out. There was some trepidation in her gaze, and he almost got rid of the cloth right there and then.

But then her breath came even faster, and he knew that she was curious about what he might do.

"Tie me up, tie me down?" she asked, his captive once again.

He merely grinned, back to being comfortable as a bad man all the way.

Jerking his chin toward the linen-covered hay bale behind her, he said, "Sit up. Hold out your hands."

When she hesitated, he almost backed off again. They'd never talked about how far they were going to take these encounters. Maybe this was when he would find out what her limits were.

And his, too.

But Nicki being Nicki, she sent him a defiant look that reminded Shane of how she'd reacted last night when he'd laid into her about selling out to the Lyon Group.

With a certain dignity that made him think that, maybe, she'd fully talked herself into the role of a fine lady who'd been waylaid by pirates, she eased back to the hay bale, reclining against it.

Then, in the most surprising move of all, she raised her arms, resting them on top of the bale while sending him a smoldering "I just dare you to go ahead with this" glance.

The position made her breasts even more breathtaking.

"Well?" she said.

He came up with the first historical word that came to mind.

"Minx."

His cock was beating against the fly of his jeans by now, but he went to her, straddling her legs.

"Hands," he said, making sure she heard the command in his tone.

With her gaze trained on him, steady, still daring, she presented one hand, then the other.

He tied them in front of her with that sash, firmly enough to mean business, loosely enough to make sure he wasn't going too far. She didn't seem to mind, though, because she was already sending him one of those saucy smiles.

"Am I being punished for something, captain?" she asked.

It occurred to Shane that maybe he was putting her back in her place again because she'd had him so off balance before.

But he went back to the game instead. Real feelings had no weight here.

"This is no punishment." He returned the edged smile. "Not yet. Not unless you decide to disobey me."

"What if I try to run?"

"Then I'll hunt you down."

The rhythm of her breathing set his pulse to racing.

"And if you caught me? What would you do then?" she asked.

Unable to wait any longer, he reached down, spreading open her legs once more. The vision of pink, of her folds wet with her desire for him, sent Shane over a mental cliff.

He was even near to bursting as he took off his shirt, then everything else. As he grabbed a condom from his jeans pocket, he didn't stop to analyze how there probably wasn't a mean, nasty pirate on earth who would've had safe sex, but this was where fantasy had to depart from reality.

But then he was right back in it when he returned to the captive. She was watching him, as if fascinated by his body. He wasn't sure a woman had ever looked at him in this way, with more than just lust, with something in her gaze that...

He didn't want to think about what it was. Couldn't think about it if he was going to leave Nicki behind when it came time.

Wrapping his fingers around one of her bare ankles, he urged her away from the bale, until she was flat on her back again, her bound hands over her head. He put his palms on the tops of her thighs, rubbing down then up, trailing back down, to the sensitive area inside of her legs.

She gasped, wiggled her hips, her gaze on his sheathed cock, which was so stiff that he thought it might stay that way forever unless he got satisfaction right now.

But there was something about her again...something that made him want to see that look on her face for a lot longer, as much as he could stand, anyway.

He slid his hands down, toward her sex, then used both thumbs to open her folds, then to trace against her clit. He used one thumb to press, circle, massage her.

"Oh..." It was the only thing she seemed able to articulate now.

"I see you've left the backtalk behind," he said, adding more pressure, working her. "Good."

She sucked in a harsh breath, lifting her hips, and he ran that thumb down, entering her with it, whisking it around, feeling her on the inside as she averted her face, nestling it against a raised arm.

Now he was manipulating her clit with his other thumb, and she rode each motion, biting her lip until he thought she might draw blood. Meanwhile, his heartbeat throbbed, making his head swim.

When she gave a sharp cry, arching up from the ground once, twice, he knew he finally had her in her place.

And he wasn't going to wait any longer to take what he wanted.

He grabbed her by the hips, plunged into her, moaning at the sensation of being surrounded by this woman, this temptation, this...

His mind lost any flow of thought as he looped an arm under one of her legs, and she hooked it around him, bringing her closer, as close as could be. They rocked together as he drove into her, ramming, reveling in her tightness, in the sounds of him going in, out, in...

Her little cries were what drove him the hardest— each sound was like a blade, a tiny edged mewl that twisted into him, lifting him bit by bit until it felt as if he was about to spill open...

A pressure in his belly...in his cock...in a place that he'd never gone before until—

Just as he was about to reach some sort of understanding about what it was, it exploded, leaving him with falling shrapnel that brushed against him on its way down.

He slumped to the ground, his mouth against her neck, and in one unguarded moment, he kissed her skin.

Just one little kiss and that's it, he thought as he closed his eyes.

So THIS WAS WHAT everyone had been talking about, Nicki thought as she played with Shane's hair while he lay on top of her, spent.

This was what sex was supposed to be.

Maybe fate had been saving *this* up for her. And if she had needed to wait a hell of a long time to get to this point, she'd say it was damn well worth it.

Even now, there was something zinging around inside of her that she couldn't identify—something light and fuzzy and wonderful. Something that made her want to hold on to Shane, press her skin against his, smell him, burrow into him as far as she could.

But, at the same time, she didn't dare be as assertive as she'd been as the pirate wench. The fantasy had ended, and this was where her life as Nicki would begin again.

When he raised himself up to untie her wrists, she sat still, not knowing what she should say now.

Jolly good time, sir? Thank you kindly for letting me walk your plank?

He threw the sash away, silent, and her heart sank, realizing their time together truly was over. But then...

Then he lay back down, pulled her against his side, just as she'd been hoping he would.

Her breasts pushed against his chest, and she sighed, loving this feeling more than anything else in life. Down below, his leg was still against her thigh.

"You okay?" he whispered, and his words stirred her hair.

"Okay?" She laughed softly. "Why would I be anything but?"

"I don't know." His fingertips whisked against the small of her back.

She bit her lip before saying, "Are you afraid you offended me somehow, with the light bondage or the threat of punishment?"

"I didn't want to push it too far."

His concern wrapped her in warmth. Her hero.

But really, she would've taken things a lot further. Should she admit that?

Nicki was just getting around to admitting to herself that she wasn't quite who she thought she was, that she'd never explored anything but vanilla sex with a man who'd ended up being more of a stranger than a lover.

"You didn't push it too far," she said. "I guess you could say I'm well-read but not well-traveled, and I liked this little trip, Shane."

Did *you?* she wanted to ask.

She was afraid to. Shane Carter had a reputation. How many women had he been with before? She'd bet that they'd been a lot more experienced and adventurous than even this.

He spoke, his voice rumbling through his chest and into hers. "I have to say, I've never done the pirate thing before. I wasn't sure what to think when I walked in here. I mean, I liked that get-up you had on—no doubts there—but the phoofy sash? The sword?"

"I think you like it when the *woman* dresses up, not you."

"Maybe." He traced her spine. "Did you care if I wasn't in full skull and crossbones costume?"

Little did he know that all he'd had to do was show up and she'd been primed and ready.

"My opinion," she said, "is that, for a woman, it's all about what's going through our heads. You acted like a pirate, you sounded like a pirate, and that was enough." She laughed. "Although I have to say that I kind of like dressing up, myself."

"I could tell. And you looked good doing it, too."

Glowing.

That's what she was doing, from head to toe.

His fingers stopped their delectable exploration over her back. "When I came back to Pine Junction, I didn't expect much. A lot of work on the ranch, for certain, but not this."

"This?"

"Yeah—the little girl next door all grown up. And you grew up nice, Nicki."

"Thanks." She laughed. "I kind of wanted to prove to you that I'm not so little anymore, though."

"You've done that in spades."

A womanly cockiness did a shimmy within her. *That* hadn't been so hard, getting him to notice that she wasn't a kid anymore. Then again, she wondered just how much a woman had to do to impress a libidinous playboy like Shane.

The thought lay so heavy in her that it dragged her down in this time of lightness. It wasn't fair that she was disappointed that Shane hadn't seen the real her at first glance last night. Of course, she had to admit that she was giving him the same treatment, looking at the superficial things about him, too.

She only wished they might have the kind of relationship in which they would go deeper with each other.

Was it too much to hope for someday?

When he exhaled, as if he'd come to some sort of conclusion, then patted her rump as if she was a horse he'd ridden and dismissed, she got her answer.

"That was something, Nicki," he said.

He rolled to his back, taking care of his condom. She sighed again, propping her elbow on the ground and resting her head in her hand. She wanted to watch the muscles in his back working as he got himself together. And his arms…strong, streamlined.

She already missed the feel of them around her.

"Thanks for coming," she said. "And I mean that in more ways than one."

Laughing, he said, "That's the thing about you. You're a bright spot in an otherwise dismal landscape."

"Is Pine Junction so bad?"

He was reaching for his jeans, and he stopped. "It's not the first place I'd choose to be."

Nicki knew enough to realize that this was all pillow talk. Did Shane do much of that?

Why not find out?

"You were gone for a long time," she said, sitting up. Oddly enough, she didn't mind being naked in front of him. It felt natural, just as sinful as she'd wanted all of this to be. "Why didn't you come back until now?"

He'd gotten his jeans on, and he didn't look at her as he buttoned his fly. "I like this town well enough. I like the life, too, and that's why I continued it near Dallas on the Lucky A Ranch. Let's just say, though, that I didn't like most aspects that went along with living on the Slanted C itself."

His dad. His temper. And she wasn't the only one who'd borne witness to it. Once, when she was a kid, she'd overheard her own father saying something about Barry Carter's rumored anger issues to her mom, and when they'd realized that Nicki was nearby, they'd put a halt to the conversation. But she'd heard about Barry around town, too—how he'd go to the Jackrabbit Bar and drink, how he'd get in the faces of some of the other men before being escorted out most nights.

It was as if Shane couldn't stand her silence, and he added, "You probably know that my dad didn't make living there easy. Let's just leave it at that."

"Okay." She knew when a man was done talking—she lived around enough of them on the ranch to have learned that well.

But she had also learned to read vulnerability in a guy, and she was seeing it in Shane right now, with the way his back had gone stiff, his jaw had gone tight.

He'd said too much to her.

And when a few seconds clicked by, she knew it was enough time for him to have thought of a way to get her to forget what he'd just said.

He hauled her onto his lap, playful again, and nuzzled her neck. The skin of her thighs and rear chafed against his jeans in a sexy, unexpected manner, and her exposed center throbbed, gearing up all over again.

"I'm wondering," he said, his voice gruff, just as it had been when he'd issued commands as the pirate, "if it's safe to let you go, minx."

She fell back into the game, too, for his sake, so he wouldn't have to deal with how he'd told her too much about dear old dad.

"I might report you to the authorities," she said, "and, next thing you know, they'll be chasing you down on the high seas."

"Let them."

The craving for a kiss seized her again, so overwhelming that she almost leaned forward, closing the intimate space between them. But she wanted *him* to want it, just as much as she did.

When she realized that he wasn't going to kiss her,

she pushed him away, fiery, crawling off of him. Maybe next time.

"Go then," she said kiddingly. "Risk your life, you scurvy pirate scum. I care not."

They laughed, and he finished getting dressed, hauling on his boots, his shirt. Game over, she reached for her blouse and pulled it over her head.

"Hope we can do this again, Nicki," he said.

Her chest clenched. "We will."

And, with that, he left the barn while Nicki grabbed the red sash, holding on to it while watching him go.

BY TEN-THIRTY the next morning, Candace had been resisting the temptation to pound on Nicki's door for hours. She wanted to get the scoop on what had happened with Shane last night, but since Nicki rarely arranged to take a day off from early-morning chores, she deserved time to sleep in.

They'd talk later, Candace thought, shutting the front door to the house. She had a lot going on this morning herself, and by the time she got back from this appointment with Russell Alexander, she'd hopefully have plenty to tell Nicki, too.

She walked down the front porch steps, her black-and-white-diamond summer dress swishing against her legs. She'd worn some ballet flats more out of common sense than fashion, since she'd be showing the businessman around the property.

His timing was good, because he showed up just when promised. It was only as he exited his sleek car that he surprised her.

He wasn't wearing a natty suit today. Nope—he was

in a Western shirt with the sleeves rolled up, newish jeans and Doc Martens.

A nature man, Candace thought. Even his dark hair wasn't slicked back, instead ruffling a little in the light breeze.

As he moved toward her, she realized that the wide shoulders she'd attributed to yesterday's suit were all nature, too.

Vroom.

Of course, she couldn't wait for him to get back into that suit, but this? This was a curveball that she hadn't seen coming—something to keep her on her toes.

"Morning, Russell," she said, tucking a strand of her long hair behind her ear. Although the gesture was only a habit, in hindsight, it could've been construed as Flirt Move Number One of the Day.

"Morning, Candace." He stopped just enough distance away for her to want him to come even closer. "Did one of us overdress?"

He'd been surveying *her* wardrobe, but somehow, she thought that he didn't have business in mind, not with the way his gaze lingered.

"I'm afraid I might have dressed for the wrong occasion," she said. "I didn't expect you to be outfitted for a horseback ride—I was just going to take you out in the Jeep for that tour. But I can…"

"No, no need for you to change. It's good to get out of the office and the suits every so often."

"I didn't think you rode, anyway."

"I've got some experience. My uncle raised me, and he lived on a ranch, so that's why I'm on this project— because I'm familiar with the territory."

She hadn't been expecting that from him, either.

"Good to hear. Before we go, would you like to have some coffee? There'll be brunch, too, after the tour." Cook was planning a secluded picnic that she would pack up and bring out to a spot by the stream, where Candace meant to sit Russell down and make one last pitch to him for the sake of the W+W—if she sensed he was open to it.

"I've had my caffeine already," he said. "I'm ready to go if you are."

She inclined her head toward the waiting Jeep by the side of the house, then, with a grin, went to the passenger's side and held open the door for him.

Amused, he took a seat, and she shut the door, assuming the driver's position.

She maneuvered onto a trail that led to the woods, wanting to go back to the community event barn first, where she would paint a vivid mental picture for him of all the dances and craft days and activities that could be held there.

The wind blew through her hair, and she pushed it back, driving one-handed, careful of the ruts in the trail. "The Wades have owned this place for going on four generations now. Our great-great-granddaddy came out here in 1855."

"I did my research on this place." His smile made her wonder if he'd put *her* name into any kind of search engine, as well.

He continued. "Due diligence is part of my job, and I need just the right property for this project."

"It sounds like it means a lot to you."

"It does. A dude resort was my idea, and it was challenging to get the higher-ups in the Lyon Group to see the merits of it in these times."

With a glance, she saw how proud he seemed.

"You've got quite a bit riding on this?" she asked.

"Only my reputation in the industry and my future."

She turned back to her driving, wishing she was as one-hundred-percent invested in his brainstorm as he was. Sure, welcoming his investment would "save" the ranch, but what would the W+W become?

They drove by a couple of ranch kids exercising the horses. They waved to Candace, and already, she missed what the W+W had once been during those wonderful summers she'd spent here with family and friends, wished it would never have to go corporate in order to survive....

Masking her true feelings, she steered them toward the barn. Candace had been out here earlier, polishing it up, even though the always-responsible Nicki had already cleaned after last night's pirate games.

She pulled up to the old structure. She'd put jack-o'-lanterns in front of it, in the spirit of the holidays. Just a nice little touch.

"You don't seem much like a country girl," Russell said, continuing their conversation. "What brought you to Pine Junction?"

"My story is complicated, and not particularly thrilling."

"I doubt that."

They got out of the Jeep, but he wasn't done with her.

"What did you do in the city?" he asked.

"Wait—didn't you research everything about this place?"

"Not everything." His grin momentarily disappeared, as if he realized that he might be veering too far from their purpose in being out here today. "I was only wondering."

Heck, no harm in this small talk, right?

"I did my time in college," she said. "I came out with a business degree, then started the long corporate climb at a job that didn't pay off in the way I'd hoped it would." She wandered toward the barn. "Unfortunately, I was one of the newer employees when it came time to lay off some of the staff."

"So here you are?"

"For now."

He wandered over to the door, too, just before she opened it.

"I have the sense that you'd be good in business," he said.

Why did it seem as if he meant…other things, too?

Good in business. Good in…bed.

Candace shook it off. Was she imagining these signals he was sending? The way he phrased things?

Not that it mattered, because she wouldn't go there. Not yet, at least. Russell Alexander would be someone to file away in her mental black book, for a time when all this business with the ranch was taken care of. And then…

Then it could be playtime. She'd promised Nicki as much.

She opened the barn door, but one glance at the area only made Candace aware of what Nicki had been up to with Shane last night. By now, however, there was no trace of those lanterns Candace and Nicki had talked about using for ambience, or the covered hay bales and blankets—all meant to evoke the slightest hint of a pirate's cabin on a ship.

Candace blew out a breath, her mind starting to spin with what could happen with a man like Russell in a barn like this. With him so near to her, she could smell his skin—he didn't use cologne, like a lot of other men she'd known. She could actually *feel* him on her, even with the polite distance between them, and the sensation smoothed over her skin like a caress.

"Here's a better look at our communal barn," she said, gesturing around, her voice laden with a quiver that she overcame. "It's a great place for inside activities. And there's plenty of land on the ranch, in general, for developing guest cottages and cabins, plus a meal and community hall."

He went to the middle of the barn, and a slat of sunlight from the open door bathed him. A tall drink of water—that's what he was, and Candace was so damned thirsty.

He took it all in, seeming to appreciate the rustic comfort of the barn as much as she always had, city girl or not.

Maybe he could love the W+W, too, she thought. Was it possible that, with some urging, he might keep it from going *too* dude?

They got back into the Jeep, and Candace decided to test him out.

"Can we be honest with each other?" she asked.

"Sure."

"I'd like to know where we stand," she said, then quickly corrected herself. "With the ranch."

The corners of his lips tilted. "You're in a good place."

"Who else are you seriously considering besides the W+W?"

"Now, you know I can't tell you that, Candace."

"All right." She tried again. "Can you tell me what they might have that we don't?"

He rested a gaze on her, sending shivers straight to her core.

"Truthfully?" he said. "They don't have anything on you."

The shivers spread into glimmers that sparked under her skin, and she smiled, trying hard to stick to business.

7

AFTER AWAKENING AND then working for a few hours, Nicki showered and dressed for the rest of the day in jeans and a white T-shirt.

Just as she was putting on her socks, there was one knock on her bedroom door and then—boom—there was Candace, who stood in the entrance with her hands on her hips.

"I didn't close any deal," she said, coming the rest of the way in and dropping onto the bed, her black-and-white skirt huffing down around her.

"Things didn't go well with Alexander?"

"I tried to sell this ranch to him like you wouldn't believe, and still…no commitment from the guy."

Nicki slumped against her wall.

"So no progress at all."

"Not really."

Outside, Nicki could hear laughter—children who loved the W+W, just as she and Candace always had.

Candace obviously heard them, too, judging from her wistful expression. "Something good will happen for us. It *has* to, Nic."

"You mean to say that the dude resort deal will come through after all?" Because with every day that went by, she still wasn't convinced she was making the right decision.

But what other choice did she have?

She went on. "What if Alexander did make an offer, but he refuses to keep everybody on? And what's this place going to look like with a spa and a fancy restaurant? It won't be the same."

"You can't think that way." Candace sent one last look at the window.

Now she was wearing an expression that made Nicki think that not only was she glum about the ranch's fate, she was probably worried about not being able to find a job or even get any other kind of deal going nowadays.

"Candy, if I didn't know any better, I'd say you're not used to many people handing you a hard time in any shape or form. But you're doing your best for us, and that's all I can ask."

"It's not enough."

"It's more than I could ever hope for."

Nicki suspected that a ranch deal meant just as much to Candace as it did to her, and not only because it provided Candace a place to recover. Her cousin had lost a lot of mojo along with her job, and it could be that she needed some of that back.

Candace smiled a little, looking away from Nicki.

That's when her gaze caught on the two items that Nicki had draped over one of her dressers, just this morning.

Nicki almost pulled down both the red pirate sash and the bandanna from Shane's outlaw costume so she could put them into hiding.

But too late.

"What's this?" Candace asked, rising from the bed and going toward the dresser.

"Oh. I just haven't put those away yet."

As if to prove that, Nicki ignored the sash and bandanna, making no move to stuff them into a drawer.

But Candace was still waiting for some share time from Nicki, probably because it was easier to talk about Shane than the anguish tied in with the ranch.

Share time wasn't going to happen, though. She'd passed some kind of point of no return last night, determined to keep everything private, especially after Shane mentioned his dad. It'd been a fragile moment— one that he probably regretted—and she wouldn't betray him by being indiscreet.

Besides, she didn't have to tell Candace *every* detail, did she?

"Okay, I get it," Candace finally said. "What you have going on with Shane is becoming serious. That's why you're zipping your lips."

"It's not serious." Nicki wasn't sure that Shane had ever *been* serious with anyone. And as much as her body loved him, she was no fool—a youthful crush was a youthful crush, and those didn't always translate well into real life.

That's what she'd come away with when she'd seen that look in his eyes after talking about his father, anyway. It was one thing to want more from him during the heat of the moment, but later, when the fantasies vanished and relationships went back to being complicated, it was entirely another.

As much as she'd grown up believing that life *could*

The Reader Service—Here's how it works:

Accepting your 2 free books and 2 free gifts (gifts valued at approximately $10.00) places you under no obligation to buy anything. You may keep the books and gifts and return the shipping statement marked "cancel". If you do not cancel, about a month later we'll send you 6 additional books and bill you just $4.49 each in the U.S. or $4.96 each in Canada. That is a savings of at least 14% off the cover price. It's quite a bargain! Shipping and handling is just 50¢ per book in the U.S. and 75¢ per book in Canada.* You may cancel at any time, but if you choose to continue, every month we'll send you 6 more books, which you may either purchase at the discount price or return to us and cancel your subscription.

*Terms and prices subject to change without notice. Prices do not include applicable taxes. Sales tax applicable in N.Y. Canadian residents will be charged applicable taxes. Offer not valid in Quebec. All orders subject to credit approval. Credit or debit balances in a customer's account(s) may be offset by any other outstanding balance owed by or to the customer. Please allow 4 to 6 weeks for delivery. Offer available while quantities last.

If offer card is missing write to: The Reader Service, P.O. Box 1867, Buffalo, NY 14240-1867 or visit us at www.ReaderService.com.

NO POSTAGE
NECESSARY
IF MAILED
IN THE
UNITED STATES

BUSINESS REPLY MAIL
FIRST-CLASS MAIL   PERMIT NO. 717   BUFFALO, NY

POSTAGE WILL BE PAID BY ADDRESSEE

THE READER SERVICE

PO BOX 1867

BUFFALO NY 14240-9952

Play the Lucky Hearts Game

and get...
2 FREE BOOKS and
2 FREE MYSTERY GIFTS...
YOURS TO KEEP!

Yes! I have scratched off the gold card.
Please send me my **2 FREE BOOKS** and
2 FREE MYSTERY GIFTS (gifts are worth about $10).
I understand that I am under no obligation to purchase
any books as explained on the back of this card.

Scratch Here!
Then look below to see what your
cards get you...*2 Free Books
& 2 Free Mystery Gifts!*

151/351 HDL FJC2

FIRST NAME

LAST NAME

ADDRESS

APT.#

CITY

STATE/PROV.

ZIP/POSTAL CODE

Visit us online at
www.ReaderService.com

Twenty-one gets you
2 FREE BOOKS and
2 FREE MYSTERY GIFTS!

Twenty gets you
2 FREE BOOKS!

Nineteen gets you
1 FREE BOOK!

TRY AGAIN!

© 2011 HARLEQUIN ENTERPRISES LIMITED. Printed in the U.S.A.
▲ DETACH AND MAIL CARD TODAY! ▲

H-B-11/11

be a possible romance, where everything would work out beautifully, it had never quite turned out that way.

But last night…

Last night stoked that innocent hope in her, something that never seemed to die, in spite of everything that went wrong.

Thinking that it was time to leave this discussion behind, Nicki opened her bedroom door and started for the stairway. "So what should we do about Russell Alexander now?"

Candace followed her out. "During brunch, Russell mentioned that he'd be going back to his hotel room for the rest of the day, 'reviewing his materials,' then stopping by the Jackrabbit Bar for a meal. I can only guess that he's making his list of pros and cons for his recommendation to his bosses."

Nicki had gotten a call today from a neighbor who'd told her that Russell Alexander had been to the Flying J across the county, as well as three other ranches this weekend.

It was crunch time, then, if she really wanted this to happen.

But it had to. People were depending on her for homes, for jobs. And the Wades had always been there—a fact that Nicki would damned well live up to.

"What do you think about a night out?" Nicki asked, pausing at the bottom of the stairs. "I haven't had a meal at the Jackrabbit in months."

Candace grinned and, fleetingly, Nicki imagined her cousin as a business barracuda.

"I think I'm hungry for some bar and grill action, too." She passed Nicki on the stairs, no doubt on a mission to comb through her closet for a smashing outfit.

A listen-to-what-I-have-to-offer dress.

Or, Nicki thought, also grinning, the perfect disguise in which to conquer.

SHANE SAT AT THE long bar at the Jackrabbit, a place that had been built in the mid-1950s, when an affluent man, Darius Alger, had come through Pine Junction with his wife, Cynthia, and they'd fallen in love with the rustic landscape. To hear the tale, Cynthia had nursed some kind of Hollywood fixation for cowboy movies, and Darius had built her a small-scale town that had been used a couple of times as an actual film set near the silver mine side of Pine Junction.

The Jackrabbit Bar itself was located in this quaint corner, next to the fanciest place in town—the two-level Hacienda Hotel, a home in which Darius and Cynthia had lived at one point. The movie set area also consisted of a dance hall, which was now a small department store, the Grand Hotel—the second-fanciest place in town and the only other lodgings—plus a general store that still sold goods. There was also a fake sheriff's office, which the town had kept intact, with a stuffed prisoner dummy in a tiny jail cell that kids could look into from the outside. On the weekends, when tourists came through to sample the apple pies and jams that Pine Junction had a reputation for, a caretaker would turn on the recorded snoring noise that the stuffed dummy made.

Here in the Jackrabbit, though, it was all true business, all the time, with distressed wood floorboards, a polished bar and a long gilt-edged, golden-veined mirror behind the bottles that stood ready for the drinking.

Shane was just getting into one of those bottles—whiskey—and he kept it near him as Nicolas the bartender checked in on him.

Shane nodded to the salt-and-pepper-haired, burly man, who also served as bouncer when it was needed. He hated to think of how many times Nicolas had thrown his dad out on his ass when he was alive and ornery.

But, as Nicolas left Shane alone now, he told himself that he hadn't come here to think about Dad. That's why he'd gotten away from the ranch tonight, so he wouldn't remember him and his harsh words and threats every time he looked at his father's recliner in the family area.

As he took a slug of whiskey—his first of the night and probably his last before he had to go back to the bunkhouse he'd elected to stay in with the ranch employees—something kept biting Shane.

His father.

God, he wished he hadn't gone and blabbed more than he should've to Nicki last night.

Why had he felt as if it was okay to do that?

Was it because she'd been familiar with his dad and it hadn't seemed so unnatural to say something about him to his next door neighbor?

All Shane knew was that, from now on, his personal life should be on one side of the fence and his relations with Nicki on the other. The error wouldn't happen again.

Next to him, someone took a seat. It was Lemuel Matthews, whom Shane had learned was the Jackrabbit Bar's most frequent customer. He had the reddened nose of a man who liked his drink, the stark white shoulder-length hair of a guy who'd seen quite a few years pass in Pine Junction.

"Carter," he said, before flagging down Nicolas for a bottle of tequila and pulling out a well-worn leather journal, immediately scribbling in it, as if in the middle of a stream of consciousness.

Lemuel had been a very successful yet low-key paperback writer back in his day, creating what the townspeople referred to as "gumshoe pulp fiction" under a pen name. He'd retired in Pine Junction to write what *he* called The Great American Novel.

Shane said his hellos, and just as he was erasing the aftertaste of the whiskey with a bite of a hamburger that waited beside him on a chipped porcelain plate, his mood began to improve—enough so that he didn't mind the thought of going back out to the Slanted C tonight.

Then the last thing Shane needed walked in.

Russell Alexander.

Shit.

And—wasn't it just Shane's luck?—the businessman headed straight for the bar and took the stool one seat away from Shane's on the opposite side of where old Lemuel was hunched.

"Evening, Carter," Alexander said, as affable as could be as he grabbed a plastic one-page menu and scanned it.

In the mirror behind the bar, Shane could see that Alexander was dressed in normal clothes tonight—jeans, a Western shirt. Odd, but he looked a whole lot less of a prick this way.

"Evening," Shane said, refusing to be broody. His

dad would've been that way, especially while putting the whiskey down his gullet.

Shane pushed the rest of the bottle away.

Alexander put down the menu, ordering his own burger, rare, from Nicolas. Then he remained seated, facing forward, elbows on the bar just like Shane.

"I got an interesting phone call today," he said in a low tone. "From a friend in the industry."

"Don't people like you ever take a weekend off?" Shane asked.

"People like me work 24/7." Alexander got straight to his point. "My friend told me about the creditors. He said they're going to be calling in your loans."

Shane's fingers wrapped around his empty shot glass.

He'd known the banks were getting restless, and he wasn't sure how much time he might have before they were no longer working with him on the payments.

Sliding a gaze to Lemuel on his left, Shane saw that the older man wasn't paying any mind to the conversation, and the bar itself was just busy enough to provide a buzz of conversation that covered any talk between him and Alexander.

He'd be damned if people heard about the Slanted C's problems. He'd be double damned if he came off to them just as useless and ineffective as his dad had made him feel at home.

"My business is none of your business," he quietly said to Alexander as the bartender slid a fancy beer toward him. Shane had no idea that anyplace in Pine Junction even stocked brew with foreign labels, but there it was.

It also didn't sit well that the Lyon Group might bring a lot more into the town than overpriced beverages.

"You're wrong about this information not being my business," Alexander said after the bartender had left them. "I'd like to work with you on this. This is the kind of business that would be beneficial to both of us, so you shouldn't look at me as if I'm the enemy."

He meant that the creditors—out-of-town banks that his father had gone to instead of the local neighbors whom he said were too "judgmental about a man"—were the bad guys. And Alexander, plus his cronies, were charging in like white knights to the Slanted C's rescue. Shane assumed that this businessman's "friend" who'd called him today might've even been one of these city creditors.

Wasn't it unethical or even illegal for the friend to let that cat out of the bag? Hell, yes. Was it out of the realm of possibility that it'd even happened?

Not likely.

Shane lowered his voice, all too aware of Lemuel, who was still scribbling away. "I already said an unqualified no to you about my ranch, Alexander, so you'd best just let the rest be."

"Just hear me out for a few minutes. I know you want to hold on to the Slanted C. I would, too. It's got so many appealing aspects, including a lake, wells and a reservoir that put your property head and shoulders above the other ones I've been looking at."

"The Square W+W has more than enough to offer in comparison."

"It doesn't have your natural resources or potential. I'm envisioning water skiing on that lake, sailing, swimming. And I see you staying on even after the transition, Carter. You could run the place. It'd still be like home for you."

"I'm not for sale." He hadn't meant to phrase it in that manner—he'd meant that the *ranch* was off the market—but it was true, anyway. Shane Carter would never sell out. It'd be a cold day in hell before he did anything to turn Pine Junction into more than a down-home place with a few cheesy Hollywood buildings offering amusement.

But Shane was suspecting that this high-minded ideal of what the town should be wasn't really the reason he was digging in his heels. It was something else.

Change—and not just in Pine Junction. Once upon a time, Shane had held some dreams for the Slanted C: he'd dreamed about improving their breeding operation, but his dad and brother had thought he was overreaching. Tommy was the college boy, and his notions were the ones Dad had listened to. Shane was merely the brother who'd never been educated partly because the money had run out before he'd gotten his chance, mostly because he hadn't really wanted to go to college. So he'd struck off on his own right before high school graduation, flying the bird to his father, then eventually getting his GED all on his own.

Now, though, he was thinking that, because he was in charge of the Slanted C, this was his opportunity to prove to all of them, even a dead man, that he'd been right. That, if they'd only listened to him, they would've found success.

Call it hubris, call it whatever, but it was there, and Shane just wanted to redeem himself on his own terms.

Especially to the dead man.

Alexander took another drink of his la-de-dah beer, and as the bartender brought out his food plate, he extracted a pen from his front shirt pocket, then neatly wrote something on a napkin.

"The Lyon Group would like every bit of the Slanted C," he said. "Every acre. And we'd like to secure it now, without having to wait for a bank sale or take the chance that someone else could grab it. This is what we're offering."

He passed the napkin to Shane.

It was a number. A lowball seven-digit figure that dug into the center of Shane's chest before he pushed the napkin back at Alexander.

Even if the number wasn't astronomical, it would do wonders for the Slanted C's present business operations. But this money wasn't meant for an investment in those—it was a full buy-out.

It would mean giving up the ranch that he wanted to make over so that it could be the place where Mom could live out the rest of her years in peace—without dudes around.

Unlike him, she still loved it on the Slanted C—it'd been bequeathed to her through her side of the family—and Shane had promised her that he'd fix everything so she could come back someday.

Just as Shane was about to tell Alexander where he could stuff that napkin, there was a rustling in the air—a disturbance that got him at the fine hairs on the back of his neck, tingling the skin on his arms at the same time.

When he glanced over his shoulder, he saw Nicki coming through the entrance, and his chest contracted.

She was wearing a white dress, and it smacked as

one of Candace's. It looked all summer-like and ultra-feminine with the straps on her shoulders delicate and lacy, with the hem kissing the middle of her slim calves. As he slid his gaze back up her body, he noticed that her hair was down again, a riot of curls brushing her tanned shoulders.

All woman.

Belatedly, he noticed that Candace was right in back of Nicki, her curvaceous figure dressed in tight jeans and a blue-and-white country top, her red hair swept up and off of her neck in a careless bunch.

He turned back to the bar and saw Alexander's gaze lingering. And damn if the man's gaze wasn't full of fire, just about stripping the clothing off Candace, who was causing a stir near the silent jukebox, where a bunch of cowboys stood around a tall table.

Alexander turned back to the bar, clearing his throat.

Shane knew the exact instant Nicki came up behind him—he could smell the fresh shampoo she liked to use. Even her skin had its own unique fragrance that corkscrewed something inside of him.

"Hi, there," she said.

Alexander gave her a nod of greeting, and she returned the gesture. Shane didn't like the stab of jealousy he felt, just because she was acknowledging another man.

What the hell?

But, even worse, when she focused on him, he almost grabbed her, brought her to him. It was the glow on her that did it—and he wasn't sure if it was left over from last night or if it was because she was glad to see him now.

And that glow was translating into some downright big confidence as she turned and addressed Alexander.

"I expected you to be back home by now."

"Not just yet." He wore a smile as he looked in the mirror, probably watching Candace behind them. "I'm staying at the Hacienda a little longer."

Out of nowhere, Lemuel Matthews leaned over and inserted himself into the conversation. Shane had all but forgotten the old writer was even there.

"Nicki, talk fast," he said. "This businessman's sniffing around the Slanted C."

Great.

Shane surprised himself by holding his tongue and checking Nicki's expression first, just to see if the news had slammed her as much as he expected it might.

And it had. He could see it in her parted lips, the helplessness in her gaze that told him her last option for the W+W was fading before her very eyes.

Did she think that he'd been working an angle with the Lyon Group behind her back?

Before he could even weigh the consequences, he said, "I'm not interested in anything Alexander has to offer."

As if to contradict him, that number on the napkin flashed over Shane's sight, but he ignored it.

When Nicki smiled in relief, the weight of the world lifted off Shane's shoulders.

He felt dizzy with that smile of hers.

With a confidence that turned him on all over again, she slipped onto the stool between him and Alexander, settling in. Why hadn't every man in town tried for Nicki's attentions over the years?

What hadn't they seen in her?

"Well, then," she said to Alexander. "It seems you have one less property to consider...."

Subtly, secretly, Shane touched her thigh as he slid off his stool. He swore he saw her shift, just slightly, and it was enough to make him need to get away from her as fast as possible.

As he left Nicki to present her case to Alexander, Shane caught Lemuel's eye, and the old man nodded to him with something like loyalty or even…respect?

Shane could just imagine how Lemuel would probably forget any of those unexpected feelings if Shane dropped the ball with the ranch and lost it altogether.

With one last look at Nicki, he made for the door, the faster to get away from Alexander…and that number on the napkin.

Then he felt someone grabbing his arm.

"Shane?" It was Candace's voice; she had deserted her table of cowboys. "Can I have a word with you?"

She seemed contrite, and he knew why that was. This was no doubt about the note she'd slipped into his vest that night of the Halloween party.

"Listen," he said, "if you're apologizing to me about being a merry matchmaker, don't bother."

"I guess it did all work out, thank goodness. But it was still impertinent of me, and I wanted to acknowledge that."

He shrugged it off, but even the mention of that night was making his imagination run wild now.

If he called up Nicki this evening, what would they do this time? They'd tried outlaws, pirates.

He glanced back at her, toward the bar, where she was making some kind of point to Russell Alexander.

She could obviously lay down the law with other men, but when it came to the bedroom… Shane held back a grin. He liked how she let *him* run things, just as he craved to with everything else in life these days.

When he looked back at Candace, he saw that her eyes were on Nicki and Alexander, too.

But her gaze was all about eating up the businessman.

She tore her focus away, offering a cheeky smile when she realized that Shane had noticed.

"Maybe you could send *him* a note from me?" she asked, obviously joking.

"I should think you wouldn't need any help."

"Why—did he say something to you?" Then, apparently sensing that she was being overeager, she mellowed. "Not that it matters."

"Doesn't it?"

"He's not interested."

Shane laughed. "You might want to reconsider that opinion."

Before he could get into some painful girlie conversation with her, he went for the door.

But, on the way out, Nicki looked over at him, and her smile told him that the night was hardly at an end.

SHANE'S WORDS KEPT ringing in Candace's ears.

You might want to reconsider that opinion, he'd said in a way that told her she was being silly and probably altogether ridiculous about denying that Russell was in to her.

She knew it, he knew it. Maybe everyone around them did, too.

So what should she do about it?

Nothing right now, she thought for about the hundredth time. Business first. Business, business, business.

Still, the words felt...empty. Especially when she remembered hearing those kids laughing today, plus what Nicki had said about the dude resort changing everything on the ranch.

Despite her worried thoughts, she went to the bar and sat on the other side of Russell. The instant she did, he brought his gaze to her.

He'd known all along that she was on her way over to him. Impertinent, all right.

"Looks like I've been flanked," he said. "You ladies really know how to corner a man."

His phone rang from his pocket, the sound of chimes. He had a napkin in his fist, crumpled up, and although Candace didn't know what might've been so important about a piece of paper, he stuffed it into his jeans pocket before fetching his phone, checking the screen, then shutting the device off.

"Always on call," Russell said.

Russell motioned to the bartender toward Candace and Nicki.

"Two more plates?"

Nicolas nodded, then went to place the order.

As Candace and Nicki exchanged hopeful glances, Russell added, "What do you say we forget about business and just relax for the night?"

Nicki agreed, but it seemed as if she hadn't given up on pursuing the dude deal.

And that meant Candace wouldn't, either.

NICKI AND CANDACE drove back to the W+W with the radio on, no other words needed—not when Johnny Cash could say it all.

He was the man in black, the outlaw.

Boy, Nicki really could've used some of *that* tonight from Shane. A picker-upper. An antidote to a disappointing night.

Russell Alexander had been serious when he'd suggested they merely relax. He'd paid for dinner and drinks, lightly quizzing them about their lives, seeming to enjoy the conversation, especially when Candace talked about her time in town with her fast friends who enjoyed hitting the Gaslamp Quarter bars.

But just as Nicki could've sworn that Russell was falling for Candace deeper with every passing second, his phone had rung again, and he'd said a reluctant good-night.

There'd definitely been no business, and the loose ends slapped at Nicki now.

Yet that wasn't the only thing gnawing at her—the other had more to do with what old Lemuel Matthews had said at the bar about the Lyon Group sniffing around the Slanted C.

The very thought of competition from the Slanted C dragged her down, because they would blow the Square W+W out of the water as far as a dude resort went, what with that lake they had on the property.

But Shane had said he wasn't interested. Even if he was, though—and even if his ranch was in the same awful position hers was in—she wasn't sure she could've ever hated him for accepting an offer. She'd already come to peace with the possibility of losing out to another property, knowing that any one of her neighbors could be the fortunate recipients of the Lyon Group's attentions.

Still, there'd be a crushing jealousy directed at those

neighbors. Sadness. Loss. The last opportunity for recovery ducking completely out of her reach.

When she and Candace walked into the house, which was silent—Cook had gone to her cabin for the night—Candace headed for the kitchen.

"Ice cream cures all ailments," she said. "You want some, too?"

"What I'd like is a nice, long bath, and then..."

A book that would sweep her mind away from all its troubles.

But Shane, right here, right now, would be better.

Should she give him a casual ring? *Hey, get over here and make one of those scenes I like so much come alive again....*

Nicki took out her phone while she climbed the stairs. Once she reached the top landing, she opened the door to her room, punching up her address book on the phone. She was so immersed in what she was doing that she didn't notice the breeze from her open window at first.

Not until she looked up to see why it was ajar when she'd surely closed it upon leaving the house.

On her bed, lounging as if he owned it, Shane reclined. A pillow was propped behind his head, a book in his hands.

It was the vampire story that had been waiting on her nightstand.

He set the book on his wide chest, grinning.

"About time you got here," he said.

8

THE MINUTE SHANE had walked out of the bar, he'd known just where he was going, and it wasn't to his own bed.

He was too wound up. If he knew anything for certain, it was that Nicki could wind him up even more, then release all his tension in the end. Being with her reminded him of the old hell-raising days with other girls in Pine Junction, except...

Nicki wasn't any other girl, and it made him shift position on the bed.

That's right—he'd improved in a lot of ways over the years, becoming a fairly responsible man in Texas, keeping to one job and being damned good at it. But he was still not steady enough for a woman like Nicki.

Good thing they just had games between them.

"Aren't you being presumptuous?" she asked, motioning to him lying there on the bed, reading her book.

"It's always worked for me."

She closed her door, leaned back against it. And when she reached behind her to lock it, Shane thought that maybe Nicki enjoyed presumption a whole hell of a lot.

He held up the vampire book. "Bedtime reading or research?"

"A little bit of both."

"I can see how it'd be instructive." He flipped to a page in the middle of the book. "'He kissed her thigh, gnawed at it, feeling the thud of her femoral artery, where the blood called to him…'"

"Do you have some kind of guy-sex radar that led you right to that page or something?"

"I must."

Nicki strode toward the bed, plucking the book out of his grip.

Shane just kept lying there, propping his hands behind his head on the pillow. "Don't mind my saying so, Nicki, but you're into some of the more exotic stuff."

"I didn't say the research was necessary for sex." She carefully put the book down on the nightstand, as if she took such great care with all of her novels.

"What's the research for, then?" he asked.

"I figured I should get to know the mind of a bloodsucker if I was going up against the Lyon Group."

Here they went. He'd known that he'd have to deal with answering for what she'd heard at the bar tonight.

Shane sat up in the bed. "About what Lemuel told you…"

"You mean how Russell Alexander wants your ranch?"

Was she about to lay into him with a lecture about neighbors not moving in on each other's deals and, more important, about how he'd chided *her* for selling out?

Or maybe that was only his guilt suggesting ideas.

"Nicki," Shane said, "I never encouraged him. I didn't even tell you that Alexander had contacted me about the Slanted C because I'd never entertained his interest."

At least, before tonight. After Alexander had mentioned the loans, though...

But he didn't like having *anyone* pull his strings. Not his father, not the Lyon Group...

He looked into Nicki's eyes. He was already burning for her to make him forget, to give him what he ached for, and was too damned proud to admit it out loud.

Nicki considered him with a wise-beyond-her-years gaze, with a need that matched his.

Let's just forget about all of it...

"I believe you, Shane," she finally said. Then she touched that vampire book, running a finger over the cover, which depicted a muscle-bound, long-haired man with an unbuttoned shirt and a look of mild, dark menace.

"Why don't you just come on over here, Nicki."

With a tiny, knowing smile, she slid one knee onto the bed, reaching back to her foot and undoing the straps of a sandal.

"What do you have in mind?" she asked.

Taking her by the waist, he pulled her toward him until she straddled him. In the meantime, she worked off her other sandal.

He recalled that scene he'd just read—the cruel vampire lord making his victim moan and scream with desire—and Shane rested his palms on her lower thighs, under her skirt, where her flesh was soft and smooth.

Power. Tonight, he was a lord who could make a

woman do anything he wanted, who had a grip on *everything* around him.

He roamed his hands up her thighs, and when he came to her lace panties, he hooked his thumbs into their sides, tugging them down.

Nicki bit her lip, closing her eyes.

Outside the open window, the moon glowed, just as it would outside a dark castle. Night creatures sang with soft rhythm, a tree's branches stirring, restless. It was getting cooler, the unseasonal weather wearing off, and the breeze that toyed with the curtains played over him, too.

He got her panties down, and she took them off the rest of the way. The innocent, white dress she was wearing... It was perfect for this fantasy, which he realized *he* might be even more fully invested in than her.

Lord. Master.

Fully in control of his destiny, at least here.

While he unbuttoned her bodice, he said, "White. This is a color for purity. Are you pure?"

"Do you want me to be?" she asked.

Yes, he did, just for the time it would take to dirty her up and down.

He only smiled, peeling open that bodice to show her sweet lace bra—white, made for a nice girl who'd wandered into the wrong castle.

The bra hooked in the front, and he made short work of that, just before cupping both hands over her breasts.

She leaned her head back, and he just about growled at the sight of his tanned skin against her paleness. The sun hadn't shone here, on one of her most private places. He felt like the first.

And...last?

The thought startled Shane, urging him to take her thin dress straps and yank them down, bringing a gasp out of her.

A shocked, delighted look stole over her face, parting her lips, making her eyes big and bright. The sight of that white material bunched around her waist affected him like a mean punch to the gut.

The village virgin.

Right now, she was his sacrifice.

He tore the dress off the rest of the way, seams ripping with soft protest, and in his passion, he grabbed her, turned her over and brought her to the bed, face down, her arms over her head, her hands spread against her quilt.

He had her now, completely bare to him, her ass shapely and enticing, her skin calling out for him to taste it.

Even if he wasn't a real vampire, he hungered for her as he'd never hungered for anyone before, dying a little inside, realizing that, perhaps, he'd been a bit dead in spots that hadn't mattered until he'd seen Nicki for the first time in years the other night.

Needing to touch her, he put his hands on her waist, and she lifted her hips.

"You're so beautiful," he said. "I've never seen anything like you."

It was no lie, either.

Best of all, though, there was a beauty in him being another person during this game, because she would never know how he felt during the heat of these moments.

IT WAS A NEW SENSATION for Nicki—being laid out without a stitch of clothing on her, vulnerable and not knowing what would come next.

Without being able to see Shane, she could actually believe that he was a bad, bad vampire who was about to take her life's blood, and without any compunction whatsoever, she knew that she'd always been willing to give it to him.

She always would be, in a manner of speaking.

She felt his hands skim her hips, then move up, under her, so that he palmed her breasts. In her belly, wings brushed her, hard and soft, confusing her, tickling and teasing with cruel intent.

He leaned down to whisper in her ear, and the fact that she couldn't see him made the fantasy even easier to get lost in, blurring the lines again between Shane and the man who was her playmate.

"I want all of you," he said. "Seeing you isn't enough. Feeling you isn't enough."

Then he nipped her neck with his teeth, and she bucked as a zing of carnal voltage flew through her. It swelled between her legs, wet and plump.

She lifted her head, trying to peer up at him over her shoulder and nearly begging for him to just kiss her… But she wasn't going to beg.

Never.

He obviously had different ideas, anyway, and his mouth latched to her neck, not in a kiss, but in a…

Drawing in a breath, she realized that he was sucking.

Oh…

She moved with every draw, hardly thinking about the hickey that would stain her. She didn't mind, the mark would be his.

Meanwhile, one of his hands had traveled down to

the center of her stomach, to her belly, and he rubbed it, keeping time with every suck.

Damn, she wished he *was* an everlasting creature—that he'd turn her into one, too, because she could definitely go on like this for eternity…

She was so into it that she was wiggling her hips, grinding back against him, bare rear end to the jeans-covered hardness between his legs.

That must've done something for him, because he grunted low in his throat, stroked his mouth from her neck to her back and mapped a shoulder blade with his lips—a damp path punctuated by tiny nips. Then he went to her spine, gnawing his way down until he got to the small of her back.

When he took a patch of skin at the top of her derriere into his mouth, sucking again, she knew she was going to have another vampire kiss on her.

And, in this moment, she wanted a million of them. She didn't care if they covered her from head to toe.

She gasped as he switched his attentions lower, to the curve where her rear met her thigh, and she gripped the quilt.

By the time he sucked at that sweet spot, she was ready to lose it completely.

"Shane…" she said on a heated whisper.

He stopped, as if cold water had doused him. Or maybe even a stroke of sunlight.

Then, as if he wanted to punish her for calling out his true, hidden name, he nibbled his way to her inner thigh, pushing her legs apart while sliding one of his hands under her, lifting her slightly under the belly. His other hand curled around her shin, raising her leg so she was bent at the knee.

"Who am I?" he asked. "Or, more precisely, who is Shane?"

Maybe he really didn't know, because she'd wanted to ask Shane Carter the same question so many times.

But he'd obviously gone full vampire by now, relieving her of the need to answer, and he bit her where she suspected the femoral artery was on her inner thigh.

Just like the vampire, Lord Darquehaven, in her book. Just like the scene Shane had read before she'd come into her room tonight.

The pain of his kiss was enough to make her cry out slightly, but not enough to break her skin.

He halted again, and that hurt even more.

"Go on," she said.

Take all of me.

He paused, as if he was about to remind her that she shouldn't be ordering a vampire lord around. But then, as if his body was more in charge than his brain, he obeyed her, adding an extra layer of madness and sensuality as he brought the hand that had been propping her up below her belly and dragging it down, between her legs. He slipped two fingers inside her, swirling them.

Biting her on the thigh, sliding inside her...

It was more than she could stand, and suddenly she reached a climax—a sharp jolt that stretched violently, pulling into something longer, growing more intense as he bit and stroked—

She cried out into the mattress, burying her face in it, an inner heat flaring and then burning out like a falling star that disappeared before it hit ground.

Her world was a blur of fire and breathless helplessness as she recovered, one minute...two...

Still barely able to breathe, she tried her best, anyway. Actually, she didn't care if she ever breathed again. She'd hit the top, and she wasn't sure how anything could ever be better.

He was even now sucking at her inner thigh, as if, in his feral state, he was determined to leave this one last mark on her. Then, with a surety that only cowboys and vampires like Shane had, he ended the sucking kiss, although he kept his mouth against her afterward.

A few minutes passed, and she heard the sound of him raising himself up, then felt his palms smooth over her rear.

"And to think," he said. "The night's still young."

She heard more movement and knew that he was taking off his clothes, and she smiled into the mattress.

She'd been marked.

And, somehow, some way, Nicki wanted to mark him, too, by the time he left Pine Junction.

A COUPLE OF HOURS LATER, after he'd sent Nicki up to the sky again, back and forth, inside and out, making love to her until she ached, they rested on the bed. Nicki even thought that Shane had fallen asleep, so she sat up, stretching in the lamplight, seeing by her old-fashioned round alarm clock that it was almost midnight.

He moved around, sheets rustling, sending a sweet twist through her clit.

"In most of the books I've read," she said, "the vampire has to leave at dawn."

She peeked down at him as he reclined in her bed. Half-covered by that sheet, he was more of a man than she'd ever seen.

It was obvious that he was a working cowboy. The

muscles in his arms and chest were testimonies to that. And she loved how his broad chest tapered into the slimness of his waist. She also appreciated his long legs, now hidden under the sheet. They were just as muscled, just as tempting to run her hands over.

He ruffled his short dark blond hair in post-sex contentment. "Is that a hint that I should make like a bat and fly away?"

"No." Had she said it too quickly? Because that wouldn't be a very happy ending at all, and at this moment, she finally had come to believe with all her heart that she *could* have one with him.

Her Shane.

She inched nearer to him. "I'm just talking about your average vampire—or at least what people think one's like. Nobody these days really talks about how Dracula could go out in the light. He was just…I suppose you could say allergic to it. It was the movies that made us think vampires burn right up in the sun." She paused, then said what she truly wanted to. "But you're not the average vampire. I mean, you *weren't.*"

He tucked a hand behind his head, watching her with a glint in his eyes. "That's good to hear."

She pulled her gaze away. Was it weird that the raw sight of hair under his arm ramped her up again?

Then again, what *didn't* do it for her when it came to Shane?

She got out of bed, trying to ignore that her heart was breaking around the edges. Maybe that was normal, though, when a girl knew that she was falling for a man who only really saw her in different roles.

How could she change that?

Going to the mirror that canted above a tall dresser,

she turned around, glancing over her shoulder, inspecting her "vampire bites." They were a trail of red hickies, like brands, showing that she belonged to him—even if he didn't know it.

"I guess a swimsuit is out of the question for a while," she said. It'd be real cute to show off a literal display of love sucks on her body if she were to go someplace like the public indoor pool at the YMCA in the next town.

"It's getting to be autumn, anyway. Forget swimsuits."

Nicki nodded in a agreement. Until now, the season had put off being autumn in favor of staying summer for an extra-long time.

When she looked back at Shane, she discovered that his gaze was trained on the dresser next to the one with the mirror.

The one with the outlaw bandanna and the red pirate sash on it.

A furious blush consumed her. Funny, how she could stand here in front of him buck naked, but it'd been those two souvenirs that brought out the embarrassment.

She tried for lightheartedness. "Candace told me that I ought to start decorating my room."

"Somehow," he said, so casually that she relaxed a bit, "I suspect that you just never got around to putting those things away."

She'd go with that. It wouldn't do to let him know that she liked seeing those "trophies" every time she came into her room.

But it bothered her that she was covering even this up. Why not be honest with Shane?

Why not see where it led?

Nicki cowboyed up, going back to the bed, slipping under the sheet, turning off the light. She suspected that it might make it easier for him to talk that way.

"Every time I see those reminders," she said, "I feel more like a woman than I ever have before."

In the moonlight, she saw him roll to his side to look at her. Was it a good thing that she couldn't see his expression?

"If I didn't know any better," he said, "I'd say you were born a woman, Nicki. It only took a while for everything else about you to catch up."

"And it took you long enough to notice."

"I wasn't here to see it happen. And, honestly, I noticed the change in you right away at that Halloween party, although I didn't see it was really you at first, not in that saloon girl costume."

She smiled to herself, even if he couldn't witness it. Who knew that she could ever feel this way with a man? Smiley, still a little giddy and dizzy…

"I haven't gotten around much," she said. "Except with Arthur. That was the name of my first and, before now, only real adult boyfriend. He left me *wanting* to hole up in the ranch office, away from just about everyone in town. He made me think that I wasn't all that special, so I retreated all the way, telling myself I needed to pay all my attention to the ranch and not anything unimportant like a boyfriend. Even if you had been in Pine Junction this entire time, you probably wouldn't have noticed me because I was in full workaholic mode until Candace moved in."

He touched her cheek, and it was such a casually tender gesture that her throat closed up.

"Sounds like Arthur was a real winner," he said. "A real sensitive creature."

"You've got some of that in you...sensitivity." She could've sworn she sensed a glimmer of it in him now.

He took his fingers away from her face. "Naw. I'm only sensitive enough to know when a conversation gets too deep."

If that wasn't a thudding hint, she didn't know what was. But she didn't want to stop. Hell, if she didn't say what she needed to now, she doubted she ever would, and to live the rest of her life with that kind of what-if...?

No way. If anything, she'd recently learned that taking a chance could pay off.

"You're a lot of things that I think you don't realize you are," she said. "You're smart, strong, loyal..."

"Me?"

He laughed, but it wasn't comfortably. She'd hit a nerve in him.

Then he said, "You'd better not say that anywhere in town. People would laugh you right out of it."

"No, they wouldn't."

From his pause, she knew that he didn't believe her, and it stung.

How could he not see how much he'd changed? How he carried himself now, how everyone approved of him coming back to work at his family's deserted ranch?

How they wanted him to succeed more than any of them because of what he'd had to endure with his dad?

Silence pressed against the air while neither of them said a word—not until he sat up, pushing away the sheet.

"I guess I do have something in common with that

vampire I was tonight," he said. "We *are* both affected by the dawn."

Yup, it was over for now.

Shane added, "At sunrise, the vampire shuts himself away for some sleep and I wake up, ready to tackle all that work that's waiting for me."

"Shane," she said as he went to the foot of the bed, climbing out of it. The moonlight from the window, which he had shut after their first bout, covered him there, and she yearned for him. Every bit, body, soul...

...and heart.

He got dressed, then came to her, leaning down.

Was he going to kiss her?

He chiseled away at her hopes once again by pressing his lips to the top of her head, then stroking her hair.

"Thank you for another good time, Nicki."

That's all he said before he left. No I'll-see-you-agains. No promises of another fantasy.

Still, on Nicki's skin, the brands he'd left on her pulsed, just like eternal kisses.

UPON RETURNING TO the Slanted C, Shane didn't get one second of shut eye, though he'd tried for about an hour before giving up altogether and saddling up to ride the east side of the property, seeing where he'd have to patch up the fences in that hardly used area.

It went without saying for Shane that he had a whole *lot* of patching up to do. The fences he'd kept around himself were wearing down around Nicki, and he'd never expected for that to happen.

She had no idea how close he'd come to losing it with her last night—that he'd been on the edge of giving more than he'd *ever* given. So he'd made up for it, maybe even in a way that most women would've found too over-the-line.

Those "bites" on her skin.

In hindsight, had they actually been little punishments inflicted on her?

It didn't matter, though, because she'd seemed to like them. And that was the thing—Nicki accepted everything he did, accepted *him*, and that threw Shane for a real loop, because how could she possibly do that?

How would she react if she knew there was weakness in him, a kid who'd flinched whenever his father raised a hand to him? A bitter, wounded thing who felt weak just by coming back to the Slanted C, where so many dark memories remained?

It was time for some repairs, all right, because Shane couldn't imagine himself living in a world where someone led him around by the emotions, where someone had the power to break him if he opened the gates and let them all the way in.

He went out to ride, and his inspection of those fences yielded far better results than he'd thought. Most of them were in good shape, in spite of his brother Tommy's neglect of everything else.

He was actually in a decent mood when he rode back, unsaddling and then grooming his chosen horse, Dante, in the stables, then coming out into the sunshine, which was covered by a bank of clouds.

And, wouldn't you know it, the clouds had brought something with them.

"Carter," said Russell Alexander, who was loitering by the stable doors, obviously expecting Shane at any moment. He was dressed in casual pants and a white shirt and holding a sheaf of papers. Shane began to wonder if Alexander also had a more secretive contract in either of his pockets.

A document to be signed in blood.

He nearly laughed to himself. This was what you got when you played in different dramas every night—a runaway noggin.

"What're you doing here?" Shane asked, although he already knew, judging by those papers Alexander was holding. Looked like they might be a formal offer.

Alexander glanced at his phone, almost offhandedly. "It's Monday morning, the East Coast is alive and kicking, and I've already gotten another phone call that I thought I should warn you about. This one was more concrete than the last."

Shane didn't want to hear it, mostly because when the bad news fell, his dad's voice would be the one haunting him the rest of the day.

You lost the ranch on your watch, boy?

Alexander continued. "Your loans *will* be called in sometime this week."

Was this hard-case lying? Putting on some pressure so Shane would jump before he looked?

"Your friend confirmed this on the sly?" Shane asked.

"Yes. And everyone needs friends." Alexander put his phone away. "Same goes for you, Carter. We both know that you'll sorely need to do something, and I'm giving you a good opportunity. I'll be discreet about the creditors for a few days, but my group is going to need an answer from you by the end of the week."

Alexander walked over to Shane, handing him the papers.

"Just look these over, all right?" he said. "Don't let this chance slip through your fingers."

Shane should've told Alexander that Nicki's ranch was for sale, not his, but with the loans getting called in...*if* they even were...

No more cards to play.

No more room for pride.

Still, there was a fighting spark that made him press his lips together, to gather all his dignity and walk right past Alexander and into the ranch house and straight to the office.

Surely there was something he could still do, some kind of last resort he hadn't yet thought of.

He tried not to look at his father's chair in front of the TV as he walked to the office, but he felt the bastard watching him from the past, anyway.

Sitting in his own chair, he opened his laptop computer, ready to go through the books one last time.

Surely there was *something*, and not just for his sake, but for Nicki's, too.

9

THAT AFTERNOON, when Candace went to pick up her pill prescription at the pharmacy in town, she saw Russell sauntering down the boardwalk past the newspaper office and toward her.

She smiled, biting her tongue, thinking he would cut her off at the pass if she started babbling about business again. They'd had a nice time at the Jackrabbit Bar, and she didn't want to squander any of that good will.

"Hi," he said as they met in front of the Hacienda Hotel, giving her that smile that always sent a shot of lightning through her.

"Hi, yourself."

Russell angled his head, wordlessly inviting her into the hotel as he continued walking.

As they passed the large, ornate mahogany registration desk, she didn't think twice about going with him. Maybe he was ready to chat over coffee in the courtyard. Whatever the case, she'd let him take the lead.

She only prayed that she didn't have bags under her eyes from spending most of the night trying not to remember that Nicki and Shane had been upstairs together. It'd been hard, though, because all the while, she'd been wishing she had someone with her, too.

And here he freakin' was.

"Are you heading home today?" she asked, making conversation.

He stopped walking next to a stand of potted palms. "Not yet."

Why wasn't he talking more?

Just for something to do as they stood there, she smoothed down the skirt of her beige dress, her hand brushing the splashy yellow designer knock-off scarf that she'd tied around her waist, using it to pep up her wardrobe. *He* was dressed in yet another different look, as if today he was an affluent man on a weekend retreat in khaki Dockers and a white shirt rolled up at the forearms.

Abercrombie and Fitch. Don Draper on holiday.

"I'm here for one more day," he finally added, a flirty gleam in his gaze, "and then I'll be off."

There was something else about him this morning, too.... Something that made his walk even cockier than normal, something that hinted that he had triumphed in a way that escaped her.

Then, before her mind could process what was happening, he latched on to her hand, making her gasp at the energy that nearly tore her in two from even a mere touch.

When he drew her in closer, she got near enough to smell the laundry detergent on his shirt.

Oh, my.

"What're you doing?" she murmured, praying that he didn't see how he affected her.

"What do you think I'm finally doing?"

His gaze seemed to go hazy-gray as he looked into her eyes, making her knees weak. She kept imagining what it'd be like to feel the slight scratch of his skin against hers as he kissed her.

She tossed her own question right back at him. "What I really mean to ask is why are you doing this now?"

When he glanced down the oil-painting-lined hallway, toward a closed door, it made her wonder if he wanted to talk in private away from the reception desk, where a young town woman was trying to avert her gaze to her computer screen. And when he tugged her down that hallway, her suspicions were confirmed.

He must've known exactly where he was going, because he pulled her toward that closed door, opening it, peering inside and leading her into a place of dimness, lit only by a long, high window trimmed with fringed valences.

He shut the door behind them.

Was that the click of a lock she heard, too?

As her eyesight adjusted, she saw that they were standing in a parlor that boasted Tiffany-glass table lamps, leather wing chairs around a fireplace and a poker table surrounded by simpler wood chairs. The faint scent of must and lemon polish floated in the air, telling her that this place had been closed off for a while, yet still maintained.

He reached under a lamp, switched it on. The beaded fringe of the shade quivered, just like the lining of Candace's belly.

Alone. With him. And he still had that gleam in his eyes—a need, a flicker that told her he knew what he wanted and had always gotten it.

"Is business between us over?" she asked, stepping away from him, not enough to make a point but enough to allow her to get her head together. "Is that why it's suddenly okay for you to…"

"Show you how much I've been dying to touch you?"

His directness left Candace flailing a little, and it was a strange situation for a girl who was so used to being in charge with her men.

The back of a high leather chair bumped up against her spine, and he came toward her, slowly, as if they had all the time in the world to sort this out.

"From the very first second I saw you," he said, "I couldn't stop thinking about you."

He was so near now that she had to crane her neck, just to try to see past that dark gray gaze of his. Her heart created tiny sonic booms that went off one bang after another, echoing through her chest, limbs, tummy.

When he bent over her, she held her breath, waiting for it….

Then felt his mouth cover hers.

Another soft boom went off in her head, behind her eyelids, and she parted her lips as his kiss became more demanding, his tongue stroking hers, his hands on her waist, entangled in the scarf she'd tied around it.

Finally, she thought.

And she kept thinking about it as the reverberations faded away, as she was swallowed by the booms that traveled through her, the pressure of his lips and tongue, the rise of desire pounding up her body.

The sound of chimes—his phone ringtone?—was a distant tapping against her stretched senses. He ignored it just as much as she did. Why should business—or whoever was calling—interfere?

Why now, after she'd finally gotten a bit of what *she* wanted from him?

But then she thought about the ranch... How she shouldn't be mixing business with pleasure... How a real businesswoman wouldn't ever go here...

She pushed against his chest, pulling away from him. "All right. So we got that over with."

"I was hoping things were just getting started."

"I think we both know better."

Her body was really getting fed up with her, punishing her with the sharpness between her legs.

She looked him straight in the eye. "The only way anything more could happen between us is when our business is done. You know that."

As hard to read as always, he kept eye contact with her, and the longer it went on, the more her body keened.

Was business over for *him* already? Had he made an offer on one of the properties in the area and it wasn't to the Square W+W?

Then he smiled down at her, running his fingertips over her face. Right now, he wasn't Russell Alexander the business lion. He wasn't the L.L. Bean nature man. He was a regular guy in khakis and a white shirt who'd confessed to wanting her just as much as she had wanted him.

"Even though I'm leaving," he said softly, "I'll be back after I'm able to make an official announcement. But I can't say anything about that yet to you or anyone else. Just know that I've made my recommendation to the group, and...it's all good, Candace."

Her chest popped. Did this mean what she thought it did?

Relief flew in her, and she knew that he could see it as clear as day. He didn't even give her the chance to ask for clarification: if he meant that the group would be putting in an offer for the W+W.

Did he see some regret along with the relief, though? The sure indication that she wished the W+W would have done better than as a dude resort?

Maybe not, because he cupped her face, crushing his mouth to hers, sending her reeling again.

From that point on, it was a hot mess of her purse hitting the floor, of shirts yanked off, of she and he stumbling toward the poker table at the side of the room, of their gasps as he lifted her to the surface.

Of the heart-thudding knowledge that they weren't in a bedroom, just in a semi-private parlor where anyone could unlock the door at any time.

And that made Candace all the hotter.

He reached under her skirt to tug off her undies, then pushed her legs so that they were bent. She still had on her bra, and he nearly ripped that off of her, too, leaving her breasts exposed.

As he pulled her toward him for another kiss, her breasts pressed against his bare chest, Candace wallowed in the flesh-to-flesh explosion.

There'd always been something there, between them…. Something instantaneous. Maybe not love at first sight. She didn't believe in that. But they were two people with a whole lot besides business in common.

Was it enough to build on?

She'd see about that soon….

She fumbled with the fly of his pants, reaching inside, bringing him out, hard and throbbing in her palm. He struggled to bring his wallet out of a back pocket, dug inside it, then dropped everything but the condom as he slid it over himself.

Then he spread her legs, pulled her closer, and drove inside her as she gave a cry of delight, digging her nails into his back.

As she moved with each thrust, he became everything to her: the city she missed so badly, the success she'd almost had and then lost, the chemically tempting man who'd been taboo to her until now...

He hammered into her, nudging her across the table with each pounding of his hips. Climbing onto the surface, he pushed her farther, farther, until she leaned back and grabbed onto one of the chairs for leverage.

Every aspect of him merged and separated in her scrambled mind: city man...country guy. The prize at the end of a long week...

All of him whipped into a montage of color and storm, each image a slash of breath, a punch of heightening ecstasy as she lost every ounce of oxygen in her lungs. She clawed to get it back, losing her mind, too....

She reached a peak just as she started to tumble off the table and he grabbed her, laughing with her, then surging into her a few more times until finally...

He groaned, spent himself, then fell to the table.

In the moments after, they clung to each other, sweaty, weak.

Finally open, finally honest.

"My room," he said between breaths. "It's not that far."

She was off the table before he could say another word. First her undies, then her bra and blouse, and she didn't even check to see that they were all neat and tidy. But, just as she was about to tie the scarf around her waist again, Russell clutched it.

Letting go of the material, she watched as he fingered the silk, then folded it into a square that he tucked into his closed hand.

A trophy, Candace thought. A memory, just like Nicki kept of Shane in her bedroom.

And, knowing how much Shane had always meant to Nicki, Candace let Russell have it.

Maybe it would turn into more than just a memento—this could be a fling that became the real thing.

In her heart, she felt like it truly could happen.

NICKI HAD GOTTEN a call from Candace earlier in the day. Her cousin explained how she'd run into an old friend in town and she wouldn't be back for a good, long while. That was okay, though, because the day was full of chores for Nicki: inspecting the breeding barn, checking on some broodmares and finally making calls to get estimates on how much she would have to invest in order to get a strong Western performance training program going at the ranch. The latter was an idea she'd been tossing around, but it'd get the ranch even further in debt if it didn't pay off.

She couldn't just sit around while Russell Alexander made his choice. Besides, work never waited.

From the moment Candace strolled into the family room after Nicki had collapsed into a threadbare chair there, Nicki knew something big was up.

She merely stared as Candace stole Nicki's barely tapped beer on the way to the couch, where she plopped down, took a long draught, then grinned like a well-satisfied kitty cat.

Nicki scanned Candace's wrinkled dress. Oh, and the hair, which was so bed-headed that it wouldn't have been a shock to hear that Candace had spent the day in an old Whitesnake music video rolling over the hoods of vintage cars.

"What's gotten into you?" Nicki asked.

Candace shrugged.

"Okay," Nicki said. "Don't tell me."

She waited for Candace to spill in five, four, three, two, one—Nicki knew Candace would spill in five seconds.

"I think there's something going around," Candace said, unable to stop herself from blurting out something, even if it was only a little tease.

"Yeah, there's something going around, all right," Nicki said. "And it looks like it was you."

Candace smiled and drank more beer.

"Candy...?"

She leaned forward on the couch, her eyes bright. "Yes, Nic, I did the deed with Russell. But don't get mad at me—he told me his job searching out property here is basically done, and even though he couldn't say what the outcome will be, he hinted pretty heavily that we're going to come out of the entire thing very nicely."

Nicki exhaled, realizing that she'd started holding her breath at the word "Russell."

Was what Candace said true?

Did the W+W have the Lyon Group in the bag?

She waited for the happiness to come, then waited some more.

It didn't.

"Wow," Nicki said instead, still not knowing how to feel about the news *or* the fact that Candace had gotten together with Russell this soon. Hell, she'd never really warmed up to the man.

As Candace started to tell Nicki about the chance meeting in town with Russell, the room in the Hacienda Hotel and their time there, Nicki's mind drifted to Shane again. It was never far from him, so it wasn't a long trip. All day she'd been feeling the nice burn of those vamp hickies on her body. She'd even taken care to hide the one on her neck with Shane's bandanna, until she'd changed into a high-collared shirt tonight.

She wondered if he was going to call soon.

When she heard Candace saying something about a poker table, Nicki tuned in, only to find Candace watching her, as if waiting for a big response.

"Wow." It seemed to be the only word suitable for any occasion right now.

"Maybe Russell already had that table staked out," Candace said. "He sure seemed to know what he wanted and how he was going to go about getting it. Unfortunately, he got a phone call to go to some appointment and won't be around again until later tonight. But I'll just go back and spend the night with him before he leaves for his place in the city tomorrow."

This all still seemed weird to Nicki. There was so much pulling at her: the idea that the W+W might be about to change forever, the thought of Candace dating the man who was putting together the deal...

"Is it serious?" Nicki asked, hoping she'd hear a no for some reason she couldn't really put her finger on. Maybe it was because she'd been considering Russell as an adversary. That had to be it.

Candace started picking at the label of the beer

bottle. "Serious? No." She laughed. "Not at this point, anyway."

"But sometime in the future?" Nicki asked. "That's moving pretty fast, Candy."

"Look who's talking."

Praise be, that's when her cell phone rang.

She stood, reached into her jeans and excused herself. In the next room, she checked the screen.

Shane?

She swallowed, coating a suddenly dry throat. The marks he'd left on her body pounded as she answered the phone.

"Hello?"

"Hey, Nicki."

Just the sound of him made her sink into a nearby chair. She wanted to crawl through the phone so she could watch his mouth while he talked, so she could let him press that mouth all over her again.

"Hey," she said.

"You down for the night?"

Down for anything. "Not yet." She hoped he understood that part to mean that she wasn't busy.

Heck, she wasn't going to come right out and say it. She wasn't *that* easy.

Was she?

Kind of liking the thought of how she might be, she fiddled with the hem of her plain shirt as he went on.

"Would you want to come here?"

Hell to the yeah.

But she paused, as if thinking it over.

Then he added, "I'd really like to talk."

Oh. Talk. Was that code for a role-playing situation that he was luring her into?

Were they already starting their game for the night?

"What should I bring?" she asked.

"Just yourself." He didn't sound playful, but she would go with it.

Her sex drive was already halfway there, weakening her in all the right places.

"I'll be over there soon," she said.

"Half hour?"

That'd give her just enough time for a quick freshen-up. "You got it."

She hung up the phone, excited about what Shane had waiting for her.

How was he going to tell her?

Shane put his phone down on the top of his office desk and sat back in his chair, running a hand through his hair. His mom and he hadn't gotten any calls from the banks yet, but Alexander had said they would come sometime this week. He thought that it might behoove him to contact the creditors, just to see if Russell Alexander was lying about the loans being called in. But that seemed like tempting fate, when, if he stayed quiet, he might have a few more days to finagle a solution.

If nothing surfaced by the end of the week, *then* he'd call to make sure.

Still, nerves had sent Shane on a day-long journey of contacting everyone he could think of, including his former boss back at the ranch he'd worked on near Dallas. Shane had pitched him the idea of expanding his business interests out here on the West Coast, but money was just as tight for him, too, and it had been a no-go.

That didn't leave much for options. His mom, who

actually shouldered most of the burden since the loans his dad had taken out were under her name after her husband's death, wouldn't be able to come up with any capital. She'd only gone to take a long visit with her sister in Oklahoma because, at the age of sixty-eight, she'd done everything she could for the Slanted C, and Shane had told her to relax, that he would fix everything on this end. She'd needed the time away—down time from all the stress of the ranch's freefall—and it was the best he could think to give her, besides the vow that she would damned well have an improved home waiting for her when all was said and done.

She had dealt with her husband bravely all those years, always standing up for Shane until he would step between her and Dad. It'd been hard, watching his parents function—loving one moment, verbally going at it the next. She'd told Shane that she had stayed with Dad because of her sons, but there'd been more to it.

Love—too complicated, Shane thought. Too painful with all its hidden corners and ups and downs.

The only choice left seemed to be the Lyon offer, and they wanted an answer by the end of the week. If it came right down to it, Shane could negotiate benefits, though: first among them, he was damned sure going to make certain his mom would have a cabin and a consulting fee on this dude resort, if that's what she wanted. He'd already faxed the offer to the family lawyer and would be talking to him on a conference call in the morning.

Shane still couldn't believe it. He might have just one week left for him to enjoy his dignity before it got flushed away with a yes to the corporation, before he sold all the dreams he'd had of building this ranch back up.

Before he gave up any hope of proving what he was really made of to everyone.

But what about Nicki and the Square W+W?

He wasn't even sure why that should really matter to him in the face of everything else that was at stake for his family.

Shane rose from his chair, shutting the window behind him, cutting off the air, which had turned cooler tonight. The season had definitely settled into what it was supposed to be.

Every movement was tense, and Shane told himself to get hold of himself before Nicki got here to, once again, put everything besides pleasure out of sight, out of mind.

It was okay to keep having sex with her—he still had a few days to pray for a miracle that might turn his fortunes around, and only if that failed would he have to put an end to their relationship.

He still had a few days to tell her that he was going to dash her own dreams of saving her place....

Soon enough, he heard the crunch of her truck's tires on the gravel in front of the house, and he told himself to suck it up, to brace himself for the sight of her.

When she stepped onto his porch, with the light breathing over her dark blond curls, the light green of her eyes with their long lashes, the sweet curve of her mouth, Shane didn't think he could ever bring himself to tell her what he needed to.

In fact, as they said hello, something strange grasped his heart—something that had been there all along, disguising itself until all he could do was face the truth of it now.

He didn't merely desire Nicki.

He *liked* her.

Before he could think any more about it, he brought her into the house. He'd been rehearsing so many damned words, and he'd forgotten each and every one of them.

She stopped in the hallway, which led to the bedrooms. Clearly unsure of what was coming next, she seemed to revert to that brave Nicki Wade who showed up whenever they started their games.

"You're quiet tonight," she said.

Was she testing him? Wondering if he'd already started a role-playing scenario and was waiting to see how she should react?

She'd be shocked to know that, for once, he hadn't even thought about what might make him feel better—not in *that* respect.

"It's been a long day," he said, gesturing for her to enter the hallway. His old bedroom wasn't too far down. He could think about what he wanted them to be tonight when they got there.

But, on the way, they passed the family area, and he spied his father's chair, which still reigned in front of the TV.

You never do anything right....

You're a piece of shit, through and through....

Anger surged, because Shane knew he could be better than that. *Would* be.

He could manage much more than his father had ever expected by coming through for his family.

Yet, now, with Nicki standing here, it didn't seem fair to take advantage of her in the bedroom just before screwing her in an entirely different way. He didn't

want to be the guy who still let everyone down with
his bad choices.

Especially her.

He put his hand on her back, and she hauled in a
breath.

It killed him, slowly, completely.

How had he let things with her go far enough for him
to be second-guessing himself? Where was the Shane
who didn't stick around too long, who never allowed
himself to care?

He guided her to the kitchen instead of the bedroom,
not knowing what he'd do with her there.

Talk like normal people?

A dull thud reminded him that he never much con-
nected with anyone that way, but now...?

Now seemed like a good time to try, because out of
all the people he knew, Nicki was the one who could
help him make sense of all this, even if she was also the
person he would hurt the most if he had to bow under
to the Lyon Group.

Didn't she have the right to know why he might have
to do that? And he certainly needed to tell her about it
before anyone else in town caught wind of his troubles
and let her know first.

But even though he knew he should just tell her now,
he didn't.

He wouldn't, not until he had no other choice.

10

NICKI WAS STILL TRYING to figure out just what Shane had up his sleeve as he pulled out a wooden chair for her at the pine kitchen table and went to the fridge.

"You hungry?" he asked, opening it, the light shining over him in his T-shirt and jeans. It brushed over his broad shoulders, the ridges that defined his upper back.

Her heart caught in her throat. *Was* she hungry?

For him—always.

It looked as if he might even be setting up some kind of food fantasy, and she thought of what might be in the fridge. Strawberries, whipped cream...

"I'm up for anything," she said. "I didn't have much for dinner."

"Me, neither." He straightened up and closed the door.

She sensed some real tension in him. It was as if he had something to say and he couldn't figure out how to do it. But, earlier, when she'd told him that he seemed quiet, it'd been because she'd actually wondered if he was all right. She hadn't wanted to overtly ask him, but the way she'd phrased it had let him know that she noticed something was amiss.

Were they friends enough to talk about deeper things with each other by now?

Before she could broach the subject, he walked toward the back door. "There's not much around here for food. How about we raid the mess pantry?"

"Okay." She was still puzzled about what he was doing as they walked the short distance from his house to the mess hall, where the hands ate and where there was a kitchen for the cook to work in.

Shane must've already known what he wanted as he faced the pantry shelves, snagging a package of angel hair pasta, a green pepper, garlic cloves and a can of diced tomatoes. He grabbed some shrimp and feta cheese from the refrigerator, too.

"Anything else?" she asked, entertained by a man who knew enough about cooking to have a firm recipe in his head.

His arms were full. "How about fixings for a salad? And—" he jerked his chin to indicate the shelves "—maybe one of those?"

Nicki saw that Jerry, the Slanted C's cook, had purchased a few pies from the Golden Crust bakery in town: apple, cherry, rhubarb.

She picked the apple pie, since the bakery was known throughout the county for them. "Looks like Cook cheats."

"Don't they all?"

"No, our Mrs. Callahan makes everything fresh." A sinking sensation weighed in Nicki. "For as long as she'll be able to, anyway."

Shane was on his way out, and he paused, his brow

furrowed. But then he stepped through the door, holding it for her with his foot as she exited.

When they reentered the house's kitchen, he went straight for the counter, setting down his foodstuffs, then taking the pie, lettuce, tomatoes and avocado from her. He fetched a few spices from an iron rack over the stove.

"You want to take care of that salad?" he asked.

"Sure. But I'm curious about what you have in mind with the pasta."

From the way he moved around the kitchen, after washing his hands and drying them, it was obvious that he was a natural here. Like many other things about Shane, it turned her on.

"Greek-style scampi," he said, getting a pot out of the cupboard, filling it with water, then giving it a couple of dashes of salt before turning on the heat.

"Sounds good." Nicki washed up, too, then rinsed off the lettuce and tomatoes. "When did you learn to cook?"

"Back when I lived here, I used to eat at the mess with the hands most nights, but I picked up cooking from Mom whenever I was around." He wiped down a large wooden cutting board. "There'd be times when it'd just be the three of us for dinner—Mom, Tommy, me. Those were good nights."

Nicki watched as he lay down the cutting board and took out a couple of sharp knives from a block on the counter.

They'd skipped over the fantasy part of the night and had gone straight to pillow talk, hadn't they? And, if she didn't know any better, she'd think that Shane

Carter had…well, a few *feelings* that had nosed their way into this tenuous relationship of theirs.

In light of that, she again started to wonder just what they were to each other at this point—neighbors?

Friends?

Or could it be that he'd gotten sick of her in bed already and was just trying to build a good working relationship for the rest of the time he was in attendance here? If she were to believe in Shane's fickle love-'em-and-leave-'em reputation, she might've placed a wager on this particular theory.

As she cut a tomato in half, she decided to just come out and ask him.

"Shane, why did you call me over here tonight?"

"Do I need a reason?"

"Up until now there's always been one."

He was already cubing those avocados on the same cutting board, bringing them arm to arm, and he didn't look up from his efforts. "Is it too much to think that maybe I like being around you?"

Warm fuzz surrounded her heart, cradling it. "You do?"

He stopped cutting, looking at her, his dark blue eyes soft with some kind of emotion that she couldn't quite grasp. "How could I not?"

"I don't know. It's just that we had…"

"Conditions? I suppose we did. If I'm trampling all over them by being friendly, I'll back off."

Being friendly. That was one way to say it.

But Nicki liked where this was leading. Lovers one night. Friends the next.

And after that—who knew?

She almost laughed at her newly won romantic confidence. But why not?

Why *wasn't* improvement possible with a womanly makeover in not only her physical side, but her attitude, as well?

"Shane, I don't want you to back off at all," she said, smiling, going back to chopping that tomato. "I'm enjoying this. I don't know what it all means, but it's nice."

He didn't say anything to that, and Nicki guessed it was because definitions probably scared a player like Shane. But maybe one night, he would clearly see what they were to each other.

Maybe, then, he'd stick around longer than he'd originally planned…?

Boy, this was a dangerous emotional game she was playing, especially knowing that she'd come into this whole thing believing it was temporary. But one night had led to another, and here she was.

Hopelessly hopeful.

When she finished with the tomatoes, she turned her head away, stifling a sudden yawn that had crept up on her. It wasn't even all that late, but it'd been yet another stressful day.

"Am I keeping you up?" he asked.

"Hardly."

"You don't have to explain. It's a lot of work keeping our places going." He was tearing the lettuce, putting the leaves into a large ceramic bowl. "But it's all a labor of love in the end."

"Yeah." Love for a place that would always be in her system. Love for everyone who lived on the W+W and had tried to maintain it with their own blood, sweat and tears.

"Hell," he said, "I didn't know how much I'd missed the Slanted C until I set foot on the grass again." He put down the knife, then gave her a look that seemed to reach right into her. "I came back here to raise this place up to what it used to be years ago."

He spoke with such restrained passion that she rested her fingers on his wrist. She didn't need to say out loud that she understood: he was a lot like her, they were both a part of the land, etched into the foundations of those stables and barns, lost without their homes.

As the water came to a simmer in the pot, Nicki felt her skin burning against his, and he eased out from under her fingers, as if disturbed by what he felt.

Once again it was as if he had something to say, but when he merely put the pasta into the water, Nicki didn't press him.

As FULL NIGHT SPREAD over the sky, Candace drove to town, radio blaring while she sang along to an old Go-Gos song.

Russell should be back in his hotel by now, and she wanted to give him a rousing rendition of room service.

She walked through the Hacienda Hotel's lobby, which was late-night silent, then up the staircase, to the second floor, where she'd spent so much of today in Russell's bed.

After she knocked on his door, she smoothed out the short black dress she'd changed into. She'd paired it with high boots and a tasteful, fitted dark orange sweater since it'd gotten colder outside. Halloween colors for the approach of the holiday in a few nights.

She heard the click of the door lock, and she helped

to push it open, softly saying, "Treat or treat. You gonna give me something good?"

By the time she stepped inside, Russell was already walking away, dressed in a robe provided by the hotel.

Someone was in a hard-to-get mood, but Candace wasn't about to tease him about it. It could be that she'd interrupted a business phone call, and she wasn't going to be That Girlfriend, who got on his case for not paying attention to her one thousand percent of the time.

She rounded the corner and found him packing his suitcase. Blood singing in her veins, she wrapped him in a hug, then stood on her tiptoes for a kiss.

Fireworks, stars…they all boomed and blazed for her until she realized that she was the one kissing *him* and not the other way around.

She pulled away. "Bad night?"

"Not really."

He was so cool that she could've used another sweater.

As he went about packing again, she glanced in his suitcase. There was an array of clothing in there—and none of it seemed to reflect a certain taste or style.

She searched for a spot of yellow—her scarf that he'd taken today, as a memory of their first time together—but she didn't find it.

Not until a flash caught her eye from across the room, inside the iron-laced trashcan under a desk.

Her mind went cloudy as she walked over to it, pulling out the scarf.

Russell halted in his packing. "I meant to take that out of there."

"What's it doing *in* there?"

Her chest, her stomach…everything had constricted.

"What is it doing in there, *Russell?*" she repeated.

Sitting down on the bed, he ran a hand over his mouth, then said, "We should talk."

"No, you're the one who should be doing all the talking right about now." Very calmly, she put the scarf into her purse. It was as if someone had set her brain on fast motion while everything else raced to catch up.

That damned phone of his rang again, the chimes bashing into Candace. She went for it on the desk before he could get there first.

All she meant to do was keep it away from him so he wouldn't find an excuse to get out of this, but then she looked at the screen.

"Margaret," Candace said, her mind a full-on Tilt-a-Whirl.

Russell spread out his hands, and she could tell by the "oh, well" gesture that he wasn't going to avoid explaining.

"She's an ex. I've been trying to break up with her, but she keeps calling and texting. She dropped by this evening—"

Candace held up her hand. "That was your appointment?"

He nodded, glancing at his phone in her hand. It was still ringing.

She thought of all the times that this phone had gone off with that personalized chime ringtone. Thought of the smiling, decent guy she'd believed he was—the one who'd kept his hands off of her until business was supposedly done.

"As I was saying," Russell continued, "she was here earlier. I was going to tell her all about us until she saw your scarf and went berserk."

A story pieced itself together in Candace's mind. "She threw my scarf in the trash. She knew it belonged to another woman."

"Exactly."

Even as he said it, Candace had the feeling he was lying. He was good at using a poker face in business, but, now with the phone still ringing and Margaret at the other end of the line, he wasn't so Joe Cool.

She made to answer the phone before it went to voice mail, but he took it from her before she could manage.

The ringing stopped, anyway.

"You're so full of it," she said.

At being called out, his skin went a bit pale under its tan.

"I'll bet Margaret was never even here," she said. "And I've got the sneaking suspicion that she's still your girlfriend, and since you have no intention of breaking up with her, *you* put my scarf in the trash. You never intended to keep it. You just wanted what you wanted and when you were done, you threw it away."

A true trophy, Candace thought. Not a memory for him to hang on to….

When he didn't tell her she was wrong, Candace blew out a breath. Stupid. How much of an idiot was she to have taken up with a liar—a guy who probably had a different woman for every business trip? A man so filled with testosterone that winning was all that mattered.

All her life, she'd been so good at picking men who had never even dreamed of letting her down—it'd always been her breaking ties with them. Always.

And here she was, a loser, but this time not because

she'd been laid off a job or had her life as she'd known it crushed.

When Candace looked at him now, she didn't see a man who was the be-all-end-all. She saw a scammer.

"I'll bet you even lied when you told me that the W+W is going to end up in a fine spot," she said, and somehow she sounded calm. It gave her even more strength. "Did you lie so you could get me into bed?"

"I never lied." The smoothness was back as he adjusted his voice, the man who could talk a woman into anything. The man who *had*. "I told you it would all be good, Candace—I just didn't say what 'it' was."

"Oh, you're a pro with the words, aren't you? You might not have lied, but you sure as hell misled."

With commendable slowness, Candace took her scarf out of her purse, laid it over her shoulders so that it draped down from both sides.

Hers again.

"Lucky Margaret," she said facetiously, already on her way to the door. "And lucky Nicki."

That last part was the honest truth.

"What do you mean?" he asked.

Candace rested her hand on the doorknob before opening it.

She realized that a huge load had just been lifted from her.

No more Russell meant no more dude resort.

But it left another weight in its place, because what now?

What could they do for the W+W?

She didn't let that get her down. "Nicki's lucky because I just got a good look at what kind of hand you like to play, and even if you *were* to come through with the mother of all offers for her ranch, I'm going to see to it that she shoots you down. There's not another Wade in existence who'll get into bed with a snake like you."

Big words, and Candace momentarily panicked at not knowing how to back them up.

But as Russell Alexander got a smug look on his face that told her he was going to win, no matter what she said, Candace opened the door and walked out on him.

Numbed, she went back to the ranch, only to find that Nicki wasn't there, probably at Shane's, so she sat on the back porch, listening to the beautiful night sounds that had always lulled her to sleep during better times. From the employee cabins, she heard the laughter that always seemed to bolster the W+W.

Children breaking their good-night rules, still up, still having fun.

Something hitched in her mind. Kids. Happiness. The ranch.

And that's when it came to her, even in the midst of pain—or maybe because of it: the memory of a networking party she'd attended at college, hosted by a favorite, now-deceased professor. He had introduced her to his guests, his contacts, and one of them…

One of them had been involved with a charity for kids.

Candace bolted up from the swing, running to her room, where she kept her laptop computer. She fired it up, looking through her files, her mind speeding with ideas.

By morning, she was ready to turn the tables on Russell and on life.

As PRE-DAWN CRACKED THROUGH the window of Shane's bedroom, he squinted his eyes. And, when he felt Nicki's body stretched out next to his, he brought her closer.

Damn, she smelled just like…Nicki. Morning musky, with a trace of summer.

His arms tightened around her, and he tried to think of how they'd ended up here, in bed, last night after dinner.

Stomach full, sleepy from yet another long day of work… She'd suggested watching a movie on TV, but he hadn't wanted to be anywhere near his father's main room—the living area with the chair and that television Dad had so loved to watch. Shane had told her there was a TV set in a bedroom at the end of the hall… She'd obviously thought that, this was it, time for another bout of Nicki vs. Whoever Shane Wanted to Be Tonight, but he'd only been tired, feeling good about just being with her, and they'd taken off their boots, crawled onto the bed, and…

Then that had been it.

They'd fallen asleep without any funny stuff.

She seemed to come fully awake just as he did, and he laughed softly.

"What would people think," he asked, "if they knew that I had a platonic night in a bedroom?"

"I think they'd be okay with it," she murmured into his T-shirt covered chest.

He played with one of her curls, watching it spring back into place.

"I have so much to do today," she said.

Smiling, he kept exploring the fascinating bounce of her curls. "Like what?"

"For one thing, Halloween's in a few days, and I promised that I'd help the kids with a haunted maze out in the yard. It's right at the top of my to-do list."

That was her biggest priority? Shane marveled at how she could still find time to be caring amid all the business.

"Why not use the community barn for that?" His finger traced her cheekbone, and she shivered.

Was she remembering Pirate Night, as well?

She cleared her throat. "I thought we'd just keep all the trick or treating near the house. We're having a piñata that'll be hung from the old oak tree in back." She touched his chest. "But *we* could use the barn again. The two of us. You know—for another…thing. Some night."

His body went taut before he could stop it, but he forced himself to relax. Last thing he wanted to do was ruin everything by telling Nicki that he couldn't possibly have sex with her when he might have to stab her in the back with the Lyon Group.

"Yeah," he said, "some night."

"We always seem to do what I want, don't we?" she asked. "How about you, though?"

"What kind of scenario would I pick?"

"You've never thought about it?"

He laughed. "I'm pretty willing to roll along with whatever your creative wiles come up with."

"You don't have any…quirks?"

Shane thought about it. "I just like what I like, I suppose."

"You know what I think you'd be in to?" she asked, raising herself up so that she looked down on him.

Those beautiful green eyes in the pre-morning light, that mouth, those gorgeous curls...

"What?" he asked.

"A harem."

He raised a brow.

"Oh," she said, "I'm not suggesting that we go around town collecting women to put in a tent or anything. It just seems that you like to call the shots when we're messing around. You like to be the boss, like a sheikh or master."

Tagged. She definitely had been coming to some conclusions about him.

"So...?" she asked.

"I like that idea." His libido agreed, too, growling, making him consider reaching on up and pulling Nicki down on top of him to start Harem Time right now.

But what little honor he had wouldn't allow it.

"Great, I'll take care of everything, then," she said, sitting all the way up, stretching her arms.

"You take care of so much, Nicki," he said.

She halted mid-stretch, smiling down at him. "I guess I'm just *like* that. An orchestrator. But, believe me, it's fun to do that kind of decorating and dressing. I didn't get to take part in much fun before now, actually. I didn't do much of anything growing up unless it involved riding. My horse Pegasus and I used to comb the fields nearest your house during my free time. That was back when he was alive."

She blushed so red that Shane chuckled.

"I remember seeing you sometimes," he said, "just on top of the hill. A little cowgirl on her horse. When you saw me, you'd ride off as if you'd been caught doing something you weren't supposed to."

"I didn't want you to know that I had a huge crush on you."

His heart felt gripped by a hand. "Did you?"

"Don't make a big deal out of it. It was just a thing."

With that, she rolled out of the bed, as if she really didn't want to talk about it. But Shane was still touched.

Nicki had nursed a crush on him.

"I'd like to stay, but duty awaits," she said.

With that, reality rushed back like a kick to the head. Reality awaited, all right. And it would probably crush Nicki all over again, except not in a sweet way.

She pulled on her boots. "Thanks for dinner. And… the whole night itself."

He sat up. "Yeah, thanks for that, too."

With a grin, she left him alone, and he glanced out the window, thinking that he should get a move on, himself. Besides morning work, he needed to talk with his mom before that conference call with the lawyer.

After Nicki left, Shane mucked out the stables, since most of the available staff were on duty at the main barn. Then he showered and subjected himself to the conference call.

Just prior to that conversation, Mom had ended up giving him her blessing to do whatever he thought was right. She didn't have much fight left in her, and who would, after years of living under the thumb of his dad?

Shane left the lawyer to create a list that would be presented in a counter-offer only if the creditors called, but none of it sat well with Shane that day.

And nothing got much better. He made calls to anyone and everyone, seeking a way out of having to give in to the Lyon Group. He even talked to every bank he didn't think his father had approached, but the lines of credit were overextended already.

A few days later, by the time Halloween rolled around, Shane knew that he was in a corner he'd never get out of. His own family's lenders still hadn't called in the loans, but the week hadn't officially ended yet.

Maybe tomorrow morning he'd have to completely throw in the towel to Russell Alexander.

Meanwhile, he couldn't avoid telling Nicki his situation any longer, just in case tomorrow really was D-for-Disaster-Day. So, his stomach in knots, Shane ventured over to the W+W, just as the sun was going down. No one much ever came to the Slanted C for trick or treating; the employees were all single men to a number, and the townsfolk had better doors to knock on, so he wouldn't be deserting anyone tonight.

He'd been working so hard to find some funding that it had offered no time to see Nicki this week. Still, he'd been leaving her messages since he'd last seen her, making excuses about being busy.

God, he'd have to make it up to her somehow, especially after having to tell her the news tonight, in case it became public tomorrow morning.

He went straight to her house, where stacked hay bales waited outside, composing a maze strung with huge fake spider webs and bats, plus a couple of eerie scarecrows to boot. And when he walked over to the entrance, where Manny sat, holding a bowl of candy and dressed like some kind of lazy male witch with a pointed hat, Shane heard scary sounds emanating from the boom box near Manny's boots.

The gap-toothed guy put a flashlight under his face. "Something wicked this way comes."

Shane couldn't have said it any better.

"Hi, Manny," Shane said. "You seen Nicki around?"

"Out in back of the house. The kids're into all sorts of stuff, like bobbing for apples."

Now that Shane was aware of it, he could hear the children over the noise of the boom box. He thanked Manny and went around to the back, where big tubs of water and floating apples had been placed on the ground and a pumpkin piñata dangled from an oak tree.

A little Harry Potter-looking boy was swinging a bat at the orange globe while other rug rats jumped up and down in glee. And Nicki...

In the porch's light, he could see that she was dressed as she came, as a cowgirl, flushed and laughing, helping Harry Potter to swing.

As Shane watched her, it was as if his world slanted, as if the axis of it had embedded itself in his chest. And when Harry Potter took a great whack at the piñata, connecting thanks to Nicki's help, she gave him a big hug before he went off to collect the candy with the others.

She stood there with her hands on her hips as the parents encouraged their kids in the candy grab.

With every passing second, Shane could see how her smile faded, just as if she was realizing that this might be the final Halloween on the ranch.

You take care of so much, Nicki, he'd said to her the other morning.

And she really did—she was everyone's compass here, everyone's guiding force. On her face, she had the look of a woman who had already let everyone down, too, and it blasted into Shane.

But what could he do?

It took everything he had to step forward, to where the porch lamp revealed him.

When Nicki saw him, she lit up, just as luminously as a candle flame.

She was happy because of him, and he wished that he didn't have to tell her the news and destroy her night. Destroy everything, just as he'd done with so many hearts back in his younger days.

He heard his father's voice again. *You damned screw up...*

Nicki walked over to him. "Happy Halloween."

"You, too."

Did he really have to do this? Whenever he'd let down people before in life, he'd never thought a second time about it. But this wasn't the same.

"Good timing," Nicki said. "I was just about to turn everything over to one of the ranch moms."

"Why—you have big plans?" He wouldn't dare interrupt them.

"Well, a few days ago, before Candace left for the city, I thought we were going to town."

"Where is she?"

"Last time I talked to her, it was by phone the other morning, after I came home from your place. She was already gone when she told me that Russell Alexander is a snake and that I should spread word to all the ranches in contention that no one should make deals with him. She said he's been up to some shady maneuvers and she'll explain more when she gets back. Evidently, he lied to her about the W+W being in a good spot with the Lyon Group, and she took off to the city for a few days to do what she called 'reconnaissance.' That's Candy, though—always with an idea."

Had Candace found out about Shane's creditors and Alexander's offer, too? Was she chasing down some of her business school friends to help Nicki now that matters with the Lyon Group had fallen through for the W+W?

Candace *couldn't* have discovered Shane's business, though, because Nicki would've stormed over and let him have it before now.

Even so, dread was hounding him. But the sooner *he* could tell Nicki, the better....

"Can we go somewhere else to talk?" he asked.

She grinned. "Sure thing. I have just the place."

She was watching him as she had the other night, when he'd invited her over and she had clearly been expecting him to be leading her into some kind of game again.

But the only role he was set to play tonight was of the guy who was going to break her ranch.

And her, right along with it.

Instead of walking inside the house, she pulled him to the side of it, where her truck waited. She jumped inside, every movement crumbling Shane's resolve that much more. Tires ate the ground as she pulled out.

Shane tried his damnedest to think of what he was going to say as they arrived at the community barn— the place where they had done all that swashing and buckling several nights ago. She hopped out of the cab, a flashlight in hand, shining it at him while she went to the door and he got out of the truck.

"Come on," she said, starting to undo a new lock on the door. "I've had this set up for a couple of days now."

"Wait." He couldn't take this anymore. "I didn't come over here tonight for that."

She hesitated, then turned off the flashlight, just as he continued.

"I'm so sorry, Nicki."

"Sorry for what?"

Shane steeled himself, because his own heart felt as if it were breaking, too.

_11_

NICKI DIDN'T LIKE how Shane's voice was more serious than she'd ever heard it.

"The Lyon Group," he finally said. "They made me an offer, Nicki."

Seconds must have passed, and even during all that time, Nicki didn't quite understand what he was saying.

She laughed, a sound that didn't really belong. "An offer. I thought you had no interest in anything like that."

He huffed out a breath, took off his cowboy hat and held it in his hands. "I promised myself that I was going to pay you the respect of being honest, and…"

"And what?"

The words came through his teeth. "And I need this. More than I ever let on."

She rested a hand on the barn's wall. This couldn't be happening.

He continued. "I didn't want anyone to know what kind of ditch the ranch was in."

It was all falling together now. So that's why he'd come back—to rectify the situation. Was that why

Tommy had abandoned the Slanted C, because he'd
left all the clean-up to Shane?

He gripped his hat. "If I could think of any other way
out of this mess, I'd have seized on that solution. But
I've racked my mind, and the other night, when Russell Alexander wrote down a number and showed it to
me, I refused him. But he's got friends, and he told me
that he heard through the corporate grapevine that the
ranch's loans were about to get called in, and he made
the offer formally. I don't know if I believe the dooms-
day scenario he's created, but, just in case…"

"I understand," she said in the anaesthetic haze that
enveloped her, even though there was something else
coming through. She was too slammed to grab on to it
just yet.

"*Do* you understand?" He was white-knuckling his
hat now. "I don't see how you could. I was so bent on
keeping it quiet. But most of all, I really thought I could
make a go of building that place back up. My mom is
going to need it, or else she'll have nothing to her name.
And…"

"Shane, I understand."

Damn it, she wanted to hate him, wanted to lash out
at him. But she knew why she wasn't railing at him right
now.

He could *have* the dude resort. Now that she'd lost
it, she knew she'd truly never wanted it.

Yet what would she do about her staff now? And
the mere thought of never seeing all those kids around,
playing, being themselves on a place that allowed them
to do just that, ripped at her.

"I need you to know," Shane said, coming forward
slowly, "that I intend to look out for you and yours. I

can negotiate with the Lyon Group so that the deal benefits the neighbors, too."

"You don't have to take care of us."

He must've heard in her voice that no Wade had ever taken kindly to scrapping for handouts. But what else could she do?

Tell him an outright no?

"I'm going to help, Nicki," he said.

This was clearly tearing him apart, and his care was the only thing that kept her standing up.

"You're a good neighbor," she said genuinely. "Thank you for trying to look out for us at any rate."

It appeared that he wanted to chuck his hat away from him in a flare of anger. "It's not about being a neighbor."

She couldn't believe she was about to ask, but she did it, anyway. "Then what's it about?"

"Honor. I don't have much of it, but—"

"Why would you say that?"

The moonlight revealed his tightened jaw.

She was still a building rumble of emotion, so bottled up that she wanted to scream. It seemed her life was a series of loss—her parents, the decline of the ranch, now this.

And...

Now Shane, too?

Judging from the look on his face, the pain of a man who cared for her more than he'd realized before, this just *couldn't* be the moment when she lost him, as well.

"I'm not angry with you," she said. "It's such a waste of time." She felt hollow, merely yearning to be filled up again with some of that hope she'd won during the past week, after he'd come into her life.

"What're you saying?"

"I'm saying that I'm a big girl, Shane. And we can still be…neighbors. Can't we?"

He still looked as if she was about to pull the rug out from under him. Any second now, he'd get skittish, as Shane Carter normally did, and he'd back away, leaving her be.

Leaving her without the one thing that was keeping her together right now.

She couldn't let him get away, so she undid the lock that she'd hitched onto the door recently, then opened the barn.

Shane's voice got gritty. "Nicki…"

In spite of his warning, she went inside, and he joined her after a few seconds. It was dark without the lanterns on, and she hadn't turned on her flashlight yet.

In the darkness, she said, "Just so you know, this isn't a war between you and me. It never was. If I should be angry, it's with life itself. So can we forget about it?"

"It's a pretty big matter to dismiss."

"No. I basically knew that we didn't have the investment. I…" She finally came out with it. "I tried to warm up to the idea of going dude, but I never really could. Just like you."

She didn't tell him what she really wanted right now—to lay her head against his chest and hear his heartbeat as the news settled in. To know that a pulse meant that life still moved forward and hers would do that, too, after she came to terms with everything.

She finally put on her flashlight, stepping aside so Shane could see past her and into the barn.

His gaze burned, and it got even hungrier as she

went around lighting lanterns so that, little by little, the "tent" she had arranged appeared.

She looked around at what they could've had.

But, damn it, she needed a happy ending, even if, in reality, it might not last. She needed to believe they could exist, though, even for a short time.

In the middle of the barn, she'd put blankets on the ground to cover the dirt. This time, she'd strewn large pillows around—items she'd found in the house attic, packed away in a box marked New Living Room— decorations for plans that had never materialized. She'd also borrowed some of Candace's sheer material from her mirror and bedroom, giving the space an exotic feel.

Simple, and not altogether that much work. She'd spent more time on the costume.

She went over to pull it from beneath a pillow. It unfurled like a dream that had floated almost out of reach.

It was composed of sheer pink cloth that she had planned to drape over her head like a veil, allowing it to flow downward, hinting at a short, midriff-baring vest, a long diaphanous skirt with bikini pants, a thin silver chain to be worn around her waist.

"Nothing fancy," Nicki said, risking a glance at Shane. "Just some stuff I bought when we first started all this. But I thought it would work."

It seemed as if he was picturing her in all that veiling, his gaze lust-steeped.

Then another emotion took over in his eyes—a gentleness that drilled into her chest.

"Seriously, Nicki," he said. "This is for another night."

That's when the anger came—latent, forceful.

"I'm not Nicki when we have our games, remember?" she said, hardly believing her own ears.

He didn't say anything, just watched her with something close to pity in his gaze.

Nicki had never done pity and, suddenly, all she wanted was to own *something,* even if it was this.

"I'm your newest addition to the harem," she said before she could let her brain catch up to her out-of-line emotions. "I've been sent here to please you."

Shane shook his head, even though she could see that he was only trying to distance himself.

"You've got a hundred women at your feet," she said, "and I'm only one of them."

She unbuttoned the top of her blouse, just daring him to stay with her.

Before he could get all noble on her, she undid the rest of her blouse, sliding it off, watching him consume her with his gaze. Turning her back on him, still keeping him in her sights as she looked over her shoulder, she eased off her bra, reached for the small vest, slipped into it.

She still had him, even though it seemed as if he was walking a line between staying and going. Maybe he realized that if he refused her, that would be the final insult.

As she took off her boots and jeans, seeking the cover of a stall so she could keep some mystery about it, she kept talking to him, knowing all the time that what she was doing was unfair, to both him and her.

"I come from a kingdom you needed to align with," she said. "My father awarded me to you as a prize, an incentive."

She emerged from the stall to find him running a

hand through his short dark blond hair. He froze when he saw her.

"Okay, this has gone far enough, Nicki."

She didn't chide him for calling her by her name. He was the master, and he could do what he wished, right?

She stood there in her long veil, holding a swath of it over her lower face and clutching the rest of its sheerness over her body. At the same time, a flash of real life gave her pause.

She was taking charge, starting now.

The anger she'd been holding back seethed in her, and she went toward the pillow bed, getting to her knees, taking a perverse pleasure in the submissive position. How many times did it start out like this—with someone or something else dominating her?

Then again, how many times had she flipped things around by the end of their games?

"What shall you do with me?" she whispered.

Shane moved to her, setting his hat on a far pillow, then going down on one knee beside her. She peered up at him, making sure she was all big eyes and lashes, and she knew that he wasn't going to leave anytime soon.

A mini-explosion rocked her, booming with such happiness and sadness combined that she finally found the courage to do what she'd never been able to do before.

She swayed toward him, dropping her half-veil and catching his lips in the kiss she'd always wanted.

The one thing she could take away from tonight, if nothing else.

THE IMPACT CRASHED through Shane as soon as her mouth touched his, and he was so overcome that he couldn't do anything but grip her shoulders, falling, falling down into the ecstasy that pulled at him.

A thousand thoughts swamped him: Nicki dressed in sheer light pink, Nicki forgiving him, pure and simple...

It couldn't be this easy. None of it could.

That's why he drew away from her, his hands still on her shoulders, his fingertips pressing into her so hard that he had to let go.

His lips throbbed, his gaze a blur until it reformed into a solid picture of Nicki, her eyes hopeful, as if she wanted him more than anything else.

An emotion he'd never felt before throttled him, scaring him silly, telling him to get the hell out.

But the last thing he would do tonight was level another bomb at her. Besides, he wanted...

To stay.

God, what?

He started to stand, but she tugged him down again by the hand. More aggressively than he imagined a harem bride to be, she pressed her body to his.

"Don't pretend you don't want me," she whispered.

He couldn't—not when evidence of it was nudging against her.

"Nicki..." he said again.

She didn't listen, instead nuzzling his neck until he sank lower on his knees, holding her, losing his common sense to a rush of dizzying need.

He pulled down her veil and buried his face in her hair. Nicki's curls, Nicki's summer scent—all Nicki.

He couldn't think much more as she tore open his shirt, unbuttoned his fly, pushed down his pants with an urgency that bounced through him, too, daring him to contain it.

Not having the strength to do that, he groaned while she took him out of his jeans, then looked at him.

He looked, too—his erection making him thicker, longer. Just the sight of him in her hand made the blood surge and palpitate in every part of him.

When she pushed him to his back, where he landed on the pillows, he started to wonder who was the master and who was the harem slave.

"Shh," she said, stroking him.

He grit his teeth as she used her thumb to rub his tip, circling, making him harder than he ever imagined.

"Relax, baby," she said. "Just relax."

No guilt...

She slid a finger down the underside of him, and when she got to his balls, she caressed one, then the other.

Cursing at the core-splitting sensation, Shane reached behind him, grabbed onto the pillows. If he'd ever thought Nicki was helpless, she was showing him how wrong he'd been.

Very wrong.

She leaned down, using her tongue on him, licking, then gently taking one of his testicles into her mouth, sucking softly. The mere sound of it wedged into him, but the feel...

He didn't know how long he could take it.

She licked back to his shaft, traveling up to its tip, running her tongue around him. Then she took him into her mouth, swirling down, sucking up....

Shane might've gone blank for a few minutes, because the only thing that brought him back was the feel of his cock being veiled by a condom, the sensation of him sliding into a warm tunnel.

Her.

He opened his eyes to see her riding him, and his hands clamped onto her hips. She'd stripped off her bikini-skirt, her vest, leaving only the veil around her. It whisked over his legs every time she undulated forward, then back.

Slick...gracefully brutal...

Every stroke was a knife in his belly, twisting hard, harder, until he swirled just like that veil did. But then he was compressing into a tight ball, so compact, so in need of release—

He came with a fierce climax, and she leaned her head back, hauling in sharp little breaths, clawing at his chest with every spasm.

Her veil slowly fell from her body, covering them like a second sheen of perspiration.

Gradually, the sounds of the night returned, louder, clearer, and Shane caught up with the panting rhythm of his pulse.

He brought Nicki down to him, until she lay skin to skin. But then...

Then she kissed him again.

Just as before, his world spun, zooming so fast that all he could do was grab onto her to stop it.

Her breath was warm against his mouth. "Was that so hard, Shane?"

"The kiss or letting myself get hooked by you?"

"If I were to guess, I'd say they're one and the same."

She was right.

Exposed, vulnerable as he lay under her, he turned his head aside, regretting it just as soon as it happened.

A long pause followed, one in which he could feel her spine stiffen underneath his hands.

Then she climbed off of him, wrapping that veil around her body. Underneath, he could see the warm hue of her flesh, the whisper of dark pink and breasts, the swerve of her waist and hips.

Again, he felt those sheer blades in his core.

"I understand a lot of things about you, Shane," she said, "but this isn't one of them. Is kissing me so…"

"Intimate? Yeah."

This was worse than him having to tell her about the Lyon offer. But why should that be when they'd never expected anything out of each other in the first place?

He started to explain, but she raised a hand.

"We're about to cross that line again when we don't have to."

That's right—good neighbors. That's what he'd wanted, and she probably had, as well.

She stood, the veil belling around her as she walked toward the stall. But then, as if she'd reconsidered her retreat, she came back toward him.

"I just wish I understood why you're so damned anti-intimacy. I mean…a kiss, Shane. A stupid kiss."

He grabbed his jeans, sliding them on. "I can't afford intimacy."

"Because your dad beat you down so hard that you began to think you deserved it? You bought into all the worthless names he called you?" Her gaze widened, as if she couldn't believe she'd said it. But then she went on. "Or is it because you never wanted to open yourself up to anyone who could say cruel and disgusting things to you? If you don't let them in, nothing they say or do matters."

Shane was managing to hold down his temper only by a thread—or maybe his anger was made of something else. Being revealed did that to a man.

"If you're trying to be neighborly," he said, attempting civility, "it isn't working."

"As you said before, this isn't about being a good neighbor. And if it isn't, then what *is* it about, Shane? Why would you lift a finger to help me if you didn't have to? Why did you look at me as if you were crumbling up inside when you told me about that land offer?"

He just shook his head, putting on his shirt.

"You try so hard, don't you?" she said.

"To what?"

"To pretend that coming back to the house where your dad lived doesn't affect you. Well, he can't define you anymore, Shane. Nothing should dictate our lives, whether it's a bad ghost or a land deal."

He got out the door before he could hear another word.

Or before he could look back at a woman who had become much more than a neighbor.

Too much more.

SOON, SHANE WAS BACK on the ranch, skidding his pickup to a stop in front of the house, where he could be alone, then mounting the steps and banging through the entry.

He didn't know where he was going, but once again, he passed the family room with that recliner in front of the TV. Even now, it was just as if someone was still sitting in it.

Nicki's words kept coming back to him.

He can't define you anymore....

Shane knew at that moment what he wanted to do,

what he'd been afraid to do because of what his father would've said to him when he was alive.

So you couldn't do anything about saving the ranch yourself. I'm not surprised. You've never been made of the right stuff.

Well, Shane knew something or two, and it was that real men took care of others, even at the expense of their own dignity. He wasn't going to lose this ranch and see that his father's "loser" statements came true.

Still, the very thought of losing his pride, not his land, got to Shane, and his anger spiked as it never had before.

In a blind rage, he charged into the room, picked up the chair, smashed it to the floor.

That didn't do much damage at first, but Shane went at it as if he could crush every word, every punch, every bruise away.

Soon enough, he was spent, and so was that chair.

He looked at it, running a hand down his face. Skeletal remains, wood and fabric, spilled all over the floor.

Then, with a calm he hadn't felt in any other place but when he was with Nicki, he collected the bits and pieces, transferring them to the back porch, where he'd haul them away tomorrow.

When he returned to the family room, Shane sat on the couch. *His* chair.

His own damned man.

THE NEXT MORNING, in a luxury beach cottage near San Diego, Candace sat on a leather couch where she could look out the sliding glass doors and see the waves lapping up to the shore below.

A forty-something woman walked into the room,

dressed in a cashmere sweater and wool slacks, her dark hair in a chignon. She bore a silver tea tray, setting it down on the marble coffee table just before she poured for Candace.

"Soon, we'll have champagne instead of tea," she said, giving Candace her steaming cup plus its saucer.

Candace couldn't hold back a smile as the woman, Leigh Brickell, took a seat on the couch, too. They both lifted their cups to each other.

"Here's to Professor Adams for introducing us way back when," Candace said. "And here's to a great future for the Square W+W."

They drank, and Leigh put her cup and saucer on the table, taking up a bundle of papers that were printed with color pictures featuring horses and ranch landscapes—shots of the W+W that Candace had culled from her computer, capturing all the memories she'd had over the years.

"You sure know how to do a heartstring-tugging proposal." Leigh handed the papers over. "You came along just as we were beginning to look for land to house this project. Your ranch will be perfect for it."

Candace rested her cup and saucer on the table, too, taking back the proposal.

Her throat got tight when she saw the front page, because she knew just what was underneath: sketches and descriptions of the W+W in the future, a riding camp for Leigh Brickell's first and foremost passion—autistic children. Once Candace had thought of how she would approach the philanthropist, it'd all come together. The W+W had always been about making kids happy, being a home for their laughter. Now, with Leigh's formidable contacts and her charity works, the ranch could allow the children to commune with the animals, bringing them out of their shells.

This whole strategy had totally displaced her anger with Russell. As soon as Candace had pulled Leigh Brickell's information from the files she'd kept on every networking function she'd attended, she had rushed to the city with her laptop, getting in contact with a friend to see if she could crash at her apartment for a short time. Then she had gotten to work on the proposal, researching the benefits of pairing animals and autistic children.

Then she had taken a deep breath and contacted Leigh.

Candace had also phoned Nicki, leaving a message about what she was up to, but in the vaguest terms possible. It was just that Candace hadn't wanted to raise Nicki's hopes about anything yet—namely, the reason she'd gone to the city—so she'd kept information to a minimum. She couldn't let Nicki down so soon after her last disappointment.

Candace hugged the papers to her chest. "I can't believe this is happening."

"It is, and I'd like to get the contracts going ASAP."

"You bet." Candace had contacts from business school she could consult with for the legalities. "I'll get on it today."

Right after she brought the news to Nicki.

They finished their tea, brainstorming new ideas for the ranch, and Candace got more and more excited as the morning went on.

Finally, though, it was time to leave.

The first thing she did after getting in her old but still shiny Saturn was to call Nicki. She drove a short way down the palm-shaded lane, pulled off to the side and punched in the number.

When she answered, Candace couldn't help herself.

"Saved!" she said, raising her free hand in the air.

And she went on to tell the whole story.

Even though Nicki was overjoyed, she still asked, "Is everyone going to be able to stay on at the ranch?"

"Absolutely. Leigh wants people who know animals to be there. And the best thing about it is that there won't be a spa anywhere on the property."

"So we'll all still be a family…but an even bigger one." Nicki's voice broke. "You did it, Candy. You *really* did it."

Throat clogged again, Candace expected Nicki to be doing a victory dance on her end of the line, but she was far quieter than that.

"I just wish…" Nicki said.

"What?" What could possibly be wrong?

"It's Shane."

Nicki told Candace all about the Lyon Group making an offer for the Slanted C.

"He doesn't want it," Nicki said. "He never let on how bad it was over there, and he doesn't have a choice."

Candace got the same adrenaline rush that she'd experienced that night after Russell had dumped her—the moment her brain had kicked into gear and led her to connect the Square W+W with Leigh Brickell.

"There's always a choice," Candace said, just before hanging up, starting her car's engine and turning around, back to Leigh Brickell's home.

12

SHANE WAS JUST CLEANING UP the remains of the chair on the porch when Walter sauntered up to him, nudging back his hat and propping his boot on the lowest step. His knee popped as he moved.

"In this fight," the old man said in that rusty-hinge voice, "I'm gonna guess that you came out the winner."

Shane tossed a seat cushion into the bed of his pickup, which he'd backed up to the porch. "It was time to clear some things out of here."

"What happened?" Walter asked.

"I got sick of looking at this piece of garbage."

The old man smiled to himself, nodding, as if he'd been waiting for Shane to, someday, come around to this.

Shane finished with the chair and shoved the pickup bed's door back into place.

Walter said, "You couldn't work this all out unless you came back to the ranch, Shane. Back to this house."

"How do you know everything is hunky dory now? It was just a chair, Walter."

"Oh, don't treat me like an ancient poop. You've been

improving day by day, if you ask me. Coming back has done you good. And, as awful as this might be for me to say, you've got a new stride these days because your dad isn't around to critique it."

Walter hadn't been blind. Shane just felt fortunate that there weren't any other old-timers left on the ranch to have borne witness to the so-called good days.

The old man cleared his throat. "I also thought this new way of carrying yourself had something to do with a little miss from the W+W."

Here it went.

"I saw Nicki Wade's pickup here the other night," Walter added, "and it didn't leave until the next morning."

Shane held up a finger. "You keep that mum. The last thing I want is for her name to be dragged through the mud."

"Oh, yessir." Walter tapped his battered boot on the step. "She and those curls could hold a soft spot in any heart, Shane. Is she coming over again anytime soon?"

"Doubtful." Shane tried to avoid the pain in his gut, even though he knew it was coming. "There've been some…complications with Nicki. And don't wag your finger at me saying you knew I was going to leave her in the dust someday, because that's not…"

Not what? How it had happened?

Now that Shane allowed himself to think about it, he'd put Nicki through the same routine as any other woman—wham, bam, thank you, ma'am, see ya later. The difference was he'd been emotional this time. He might not even have left her if she hadn't forced him out with all that honesty about his father.

Walter lowered his tone. "Then tell me what did happen to get you all riled up like this."

Shane wasn't about to say a word about Nicki.

So he went ahead and told Walter about the money possibly being called in—maybe even today—and what he'd have to do with the ranch. If what Russell Alexander had told him was true, then everyone was about to find out, anyway, and Walter deserved to be one of the first to hear the news.

"All I've got now," Shane said, "is the need to negotiate with the Lyon Group. Mom would still like this house and a patch of property to go with it, if the group will agree to that."

"Really?" Walter said sarcastically. "That's all you've got now is a fighting spirit?"

When Shane hitched his thumbs into his belt loops, Walter chuffed.

"I watched you throughout the years, going from a little scamp to an oversexed teenager," he said. "I saw a lot I didn't like about your growing up—the way your dad treated you, the way he drove you off with his attitude and actions. It'd be a shame to see you run off from this ranch again, especially after you've matured enough to shove all that negativity right back at Barry Carter, whether he sees it or not. He ain't here now, but it counts, Shane. Believe that."

Shane lowered his hands from his belt loops. "How much of a choice is there? What else is there to do besides give the Lyon Group what they want? I'm not going to leave anyone on this ranch in the lurch by refusing an offer that won't come from anyone else."

"Boy, have you bothered to look around you to see what's really here?"

Shane had no idea what that meant.

Walter rolled his eyes. "I'm not blind. I knew how this place was faring, but I didn't stick my nose deep into matters when you came along. You were perfectly capable. Knowing what I know now, though, I'd suggest to you that this Russell Alexander character might have some sway with your creditors."

"Are you intimating that, if he's not lying about the loans outright, he's using the creditors to put pressure on me?"

Walter shrugged. "Whatever the case is, you've got avenues right here in town that you might not have considered."

Bristling, Shane asked, "What do you mean?"

"Everyone hasn't been blind to the economics. Tommy sold off a lot of our stock, laid off a lot of the staff. He was like your father, you know—uncaring about the families on the Slanted C. When you came back, people started talking, and there was a general sense of…"

"What?"

"Well, that things could change, and that they would help you with that if you needed it. All you have to do is reach out to a few folks, Shane, even if the thought of it kills you."

Shane fisted his hands by his side as Walter went on.

"Lemuel Matthews, for one, has a real nest egg. He socked away a lot of money from those detective novels he wrote. I have a bit tucked away, too. Not enough to cover what you have to manage here, but…"

He trailed off, and Shane burned with mortification.

He was even a little stunned. No one cared that he might not be man enough to raise the Slanted C up again?

They wanted to *help?*

"You just have to say something," Walter said. "Unless you're just as bullheaded as that dead dad of yours."

Walter gave a pointed glance to the destroyed chair in the pickup, insinuating that Shane would probably rather trash the house than settle into it as a legacy of Barry Carter.

As the older man walked away, optimism rose in Shane's chest, probably for the first time in his life. If he swallowed his pride, calling on Lemuel, there might be a chance in hell of hope...

Then he could get in touch with Russell Alexander. And when Alexander heard Shane's rejection, why...

Shane exhaled. The Lyon Group might just make an offer to Nicki, and she could either have the satisfaction of turning the snake down or getting all she could out of him, although he doubted it with what Candace had told her.

But that would be all that Shane could give her. He only wished it could be more.

He could hardly believe it—Shane Carter, the world's worst candidate for affection finally had a meaningful crush.

It sounded like a *good* thing, but he knew in his heart that, underneath every role he'd played with her, he'd only been a true disaster after being stripped down to the bare essentials last night. Why should he expect himself to be anything else in the future?

He went inside the house, and even as the sun shone

over the hills, there was a dark sore patch that remained right in the center of him.

Right where he was trying to forget Nicki.

Even when he got the call from Candace, he was still hurting, although what she had to say should've lessened the pain.

NICKI WAS ON PINS and needles as she put together lunch for Candace and her, slathering crusty rolls with mayonnaise and layering them with cheeses, veggies and lunch meats.

She should be over the moon, with Candace's last-minute save for both the W+W and now, maybe, possibly, the Slanted C. And she might've been if only her every thought wasn't tinged by Shane himself.

Even now, what had happened between them last night made her stomach churn.

In fact, she had stayed up all night, thinking of what she'd said to Shane in the barn about his dad. Would he ever forgive her?

Good God, maybe a better question was if he would ever want to be near her again.

Almost mindlessly, she plated the sandwiches and brought them to the small kitchen table. She was just getting a couple of celebratory orange sodas out of the fridge when Candace barged in through the back porch door, the screen banging against the frame.

"It's a beautiful day!" she said, raising her hands above her head, her fashion-plate leather work bag swinging from her shoulder.

She looked like a winner, in her red business suit and stylish two-toned pumps. But Candace had always been that way—she didn't have to just dress the part.

Nicki smiled, rushing to Candace to give her a big, thankful bear hug.

"Whoa," Candace said, laughing, pulling away.

"I missed you while you were gone," Nicki said, sitting at the table.

Candace followed. "Same here."

While she gave Nicki a fond look, she zeroed in on her, too, as if peeking into what really lay beneath.

Nicki wasn't about to ruin this. She should be cheering, damn it.

"Did you call Shane?" she asked, his name catching in her chest.

"You bet I did, but only after I talked to Leigh about the possibility of putting both of our ranches together. She was ecstatic. She's already got plans for the Slanted C's lake. Can you imagine what kind of fun those kids will have with it?"

Nicki nodded, unable to speak. Their ranches, joined. They could be more than neighbors or...whatever they were or weren't to each other now.

"He sounded relieved," Candace said, "just as much as I was when I realized we weren't going to have to go dude. Just as much as you, too, I imagine."

"So he's on board."

"He's definitely on board." Candace hugged Nicki this time, her words muffled by Nicki's hair. "This all happened so fast, and I didn't want to let you in on the details until I knew that Leigh was interested. I didn't want to raise your hopes because, Lord knows, you've had enough to deal with."

Nicki squeezed Candace all the harder, until they pulled back from each other.

"Survivors," Nicki said.

"All of us, together." Candace eyed the sandwiches on the table, as if she were famished. "I just wish I could see Russell Alexander's face when the paperwork comes through. Heck—I wish I could gloat in front of him right now, after Shane calls him and tells him to stick his offer where the sun don't shine. Did you know Russell came up with the whole dude resort idea? This setback's going to smart for him."

"What exactly did he do to you?" Nicki asked. "You never really told me."

Candace narrowed her eyes. "When he implied that he'd chosen the W+W, it was only because he wanted to get me in to bed. I know that now because, that night, when I went back to him at the hotel, he dropped me like yesterday's boxers. But he's the one who got my brain in gear, so we should actually thank the jerk."

Nicki wished she could find a way to make Shane not sting so much, too.

They dug into the sandwiches. Or, at least, Candace did, her appetite hearty, while Nicki slowly ate her food. All the while, though, Candace seemed restless, as if she had so many more ideas swirling around in her head.

Nicki knew she was right when Candace suddenly wiped her mouth with her napkin and stood. "I have no idea why I'm just sitting here when there's an opportunity right in front of my face. I'm going to show him that he didn't win."

She went for the door.

"Candy...?"

"I'll be back before dinner."

When Candace sent Nicki a sweet, razor-edged smile, Nicki knew that Russell Alexander was in trouble.

She kept sitting at the kitchen table while Candace's words played back to her.

I have no idea why I'm just sitting here when there's an opportunity right in front of my face....

Hadn't she been fighting back lately, too, until last night, when all her hopes had come crashing down around her?

She'd successfully made her way out from behind those ledgers and accounting columns that had held her at bay for so many years, so was she going to let one bad night put an end to her and Shane's relationship?

But a snag of doubt held her back from running out of the kitchen and going to her truck, which could take her to Shane's place. That "argument" last night had been about a lot more than merely a trifle. Besides her need to strike out, Shane hadn't wanted intimacy. That was huge. And putting herself out there for him when she knew he would probably refuse her...

It would mean stepping entirely out of the fantasies they'd created, offering herself and nothing more to him.

Would that be enough?

Nicki glanced toward the counter, where she'd set one of her books the other day—the vampire story from which Shane had taken inspiration.

A happy ending waiting for her to either read it...

Or live it.

CANDACE HAD NEVER driven anywhere so fast in her life. She was lucky she didn't get a speeding ticket.

But it must've been her lucky day.

She arrived in record time in downtown San Diego, where she knew the Lyon Group had offices in one of the skyscrapers that glimmered in the late-afternoon sun. She parked, then took an elevator up to the lobby and checked the reception area to see which offices were on what floor.

Then she took the stairs to the third level.

The young woman behind the reception desk there greeted Candace as she peered around at the glass offices.

In one of them, she found just the person she'd come here to see.

She headed toward him before the receptionist could stop her, then stood in the doorway until Russell Alexander swiveled around in his desk chair. He was dressed in a slick suit, just like the first time she'd seen him.

Aw, poor baby looked sad right now. He must've already gotten Shane's phone call.

"Hello," Candace said, trying hard not to gloat. Yet.

She would definitely be doing some of that after all the papers were signed, but right now, she just wanted Russell to get a good look at her. Wanted to plant the seed in him so he'd know who'd gotten Shane to make that call, know exactly who had undercut him and stolen the Slanted C right from under his nose.

She wanted him to know that he'd never realized just whom he'd been dealing with.

He put down that infernal phone of his; he'd been texting someone. Probably poor Margaret.

The receptionist came up behind Candace, who spoke over her shoulder to her.

"I'll only be a moment."

Russell nodded to the girl, then gave Candace a cool glance. "I've already heard," he said. "Are you here to rub it in?"

"No, I actually just wanted to thank you," she said.

She could see the exact moment that confusion struck his pea brain.

"For what?" he asked.

"For giving me the kind of inspiration I never would've had if you hadn't kicked me to the curb."

Short, sweet, memorable. She had no more to say, and she turned around, knowing that she'd hold dear to the sight of him looking so confused for as long as she lived.

"Candace?" he asked as she left him behind.

She took the stairs, not bothering to answer him, content with the notion that, with the lucky day she was having, he'd be on the bottom of the company totem pole by quitting time, and he'd remember damn well who'd put him there.

THAT EVENING, when Shane heard tires crunching over gravel outside the house, he put down the knife he was using to slice up some green beans for dinner.

Nicki?

She was at his back door, opening it and stepping inside before he could even invite her.

But from the way his heart was rolling through him, he wondered if he would've kept her out, anyway.

Flushed, she just stood there in her flannel cowgirl shirt and jeans and ponytailed hair, as if the very act of seeing him had punched her in the gut and made her forget what she was going to say.

Hell, she wasn't the only one.

But the longer their tense silence stretched, the more aware he became that maybe she wasn't here for a social call. It had to be about the business of the day.

How could he have thought any differently, especially after last night?

She swallowed. "It took me a few hours to come here."

Why? Had she been collecting her courage?

He took the chance to put himself back together, too, then veered as far away as he could from why she might've needed courage to see him. "It seems we're going to be partners."

Nicki's gaze lost some of its shine, but then she raised her chin. "So what do you think?"

He couldn't stand another hour without her—that's what he thought.

Instead, he said, "Since Leigh Brickell told me that she'd like to keep my staff on, and that my mom would get this house plus a parcel of land for her retirement, it sounds like a fine deal to me. Plus, it's for a greater cause than I could've ever come up with."

"I think so, too."

Bruised. That was the color of her words, and he'd been the one to do that to her.

But then something happened to Nicki—a gradual strength that filled her eyes.

"We'll be able to work together, right?"

Bam—she'd nailed him once again. But the thing was that she didn't turn her back on him. She hadn't done it last night, either, because he'd left first.

As usual.

She took a step toward him. "You're not going to withdraw and get all stubborn on me—"

"Nicki, last night you said that Barry Carter shouldn't define me, and he's not going to do it today. I'm not anything like him."

No anger in him, just…the truth.

And she heard it. He could tell by the sheen in her eyes, the way she looked at him as if she was really seeing him for the first time, as the man he was, not a youthful crush or a character in a scene.

As a guy who'd found his footing.

"We're going to work together just fine," he said.

"We are?"

She'd gotten some kind of extra meaning from his comment, and he realized that he meant it with every cell in his body.

Nicki *should* be here, with him, today…and tonight….

Maybe even longer than that?

He moved from the counter, toward Nicki, only a few long steps away from her, and she pressed her lips together, as if she was attempting to hold in her emotions.

Then she spoke. "All I ever wanted was to…work… together with you, Shane."

This was too good to be true, he thought. Even with what she'd just said, the injuries of the past kept reminding him that being vulnerable could lead to him retreating behind an emotional wall so he could stay intact.

Like in everything else, Nicki could clearly tell he was still struggling, and she kept a slight distance.

"I'm not sure what to do next with you—not without a costume," Nicki began. She shook her head. "Maybe that's not true, though, because last night, even when I was wearing that harem girl outfit, I wasn't disguising what I felt. In fact, I don't think I've *ever* worn a costume with you."

Was she waiting for him to admit the same? Well, he

couldn't. He'd enveloped himself in the power of those roles too deeply.

"Shane, whenever you let down your guard with me, those are the times I knew what I wanted from you. And whenever you dropped those shields, I saw you as a strong man, not a weak one."

"That's not what I learned over the years." Shields were good.

At least, they had been before now.

Nicki sighed. "You know that you just can't go through life trying to please someone who doesn't even exist."

Like all the unreal people she'd played?

Or was she talking about his father again?

"What matters," she said, "is that I want to be with you, in spite of when or where or why it is. Don't you get that?" She tilted her head at a heartbreaking slant. "Didn't you ever get it?"

She was telling him things that he'd never heard from anyone in his life. He'd never allowed women the chance, and that had almost been the case with Nicki, too.

He hadn't responded yet, and he wondered how long it would take before she turned around and wrote him off. But she was what mattered most to him.

What would come next, if he allowed *that*?

He deliberately walked the rest of the way to her, and her gaze widened. He fell into the light green of her eyes just before he closed his own and pressed his lips to hers.

At first, it was as if she couldn't believe he was kissing her when he'd never done it willingly before. She'd attempted to steal one from him last night, but he'd given her little in response. But now, as he wrapped his arms around her and pulled her in, his lips said everything.

I'm yours.

Shane Carter is all *yours, Nicki Wade.*

He sipped at her, slowly, enjoying the softness of her mouth, the way she made a tiny sound of happiness beneath his own lips.

When he'd made his point, he kept hold of her, using one hand to stroke her cheek with his fingertips.

"I do get it," he said.

She smiled, her eyes glassy. "I can see that now."

He kissed her again, with more promise this time—vows of long nights ahead spent in each other's arms and dreams of him being there way after the sun came up, every day.

Every night.

Epilogue

THE DAY THAT Nicki and Shane knocked down a part of the fence that separated the Square W+W from the Slanted C was crisp, with storm clouds riding on the horizon. Still, everyone had shown up for the festivities in spite of the weather.

As the couple pushed at the already loosened fencing, it gave way, crashing to the grass with a puff of dirt. On both sides of what used to be a divide, both sets of employees and families clapped and whooped while Candace hiked up her skirt, then stamped her fashionable red pump down on the wood and raised a fist in victory.

The cheers got even louder before most of the crowd headed for the food spread that the combined ranches had set out under a large tent—a precaution just in case the weather report had been all too correct and rain came down.

Shane, Nicki, Candace and Leigh Brickell remained behind.

Leigh popped open a bottle of Cristal, and as it frothed bubbles, Candace picked up flutes from the ground and held them under the streams of champagne, giving one to each of them.

They raised their glasses, and Leigh toasted first.

"To the group who made this groundbreaking possible. Long live the Circle C+W Ranch!"

"And," Candace said, "here's to everyone else who made this possible."

She didn't have to say the name when they all knew it.

Russell Alexander, who, according to business gossip, had left the Lyon Group and moved out of state. His bosses at the group had never really been on board with the whole dude resort idea, and they had decided to nix the entire project when the Slanted C had become unavailable.

Candace and Leigh went bottoms up with the champagne, but Shane and Nicki merely looked at each other. It didn't take much to get lost in his gaze, Nicki thought, already drowning in the blue of his eyes.

They clinked glasses, then drank.

Candace was wearing one of her typically bright business suits that she'd purchased for her new job working with Leigh, developing land from other ranches around the county in anticipation of other philanthropic projects. She wandered with her new mentor toward the food. Already, the ranch kids were digging into the cotton candy from the dessert stand, and mothers were dragging them to the healthier stuff.

It wasn't too long ago that Nicki would've felt less attractive next to her high-flying cousin, but these days…?

Not so much.

Even though she was in a simple wool skirt, sweater

and her boots, Shane looked at her as if she had materialized from the most enticed parts of his brain.

She didn't have to dress up to be his princess or whatever was going on in that mind of his today.

"Not that I don't want to celebrate," he said, "but I can't get you alone fast enough."

Not a week went by that they didn't joke about what had brought them together—the games, the different roles, the great sex.

Of course, they still had a lot of that last part going on. The games, though, were occasional.

The sky rumbled, letting them know that the rain had held off for as long as it wanted to and they should be prepared.

"Enough of this," he said, starting to toss out the rest of his champagne before Nicki stopped him, taking his glass.

"What're you doing?" she asked.

"Getting ready for my mom to come in from the airport. She'll be ticked that I started on the bubbly without her."

How true that would be. Nicki had reacquainted herself with his mom when the woman had paid a visit. She had wanted to meet Shane's girlfriend before she gave up her long vacation out of town altogether and moved back into her house on a ranch that would be ready for campers come summer. Nicki and she had gotten on like fast pals over a less expensive version of champagne one night.

The woman did like her bubbly, now that life had improved for her.

"There'll be some champagne in the limo Leigh's

sending," Nicki said, "so don't sweat it. I just wish your mom could've been here for the fence-crashing."

"We waited as long as possible, but the rain's going to beat her."

"Yeah, but…"

Shane had gotten serious, and Nicki went quiet. Something was definitely going on with him.

"What?" she asked.

"I don't know." He traced his fingers over her cheekbone, her neck, her sweater-clad shoulder, as if inspecting her. "There's just…*something* missing from this noteworthy day."

"Shane…"

He took one of the champagne glasses from her, then held her hand, running his thumb over her ring finger.

When he let go of her hand and reached into a pocket to fetch a golden band with diamond sparkle, then slid it onto her finger, her breath caught. Something caught in her throat, too, barring words. Burning.

"That's what was missing," he said softly.

She held up her hand, held back tears, as well.

"Are you commanding me to marry you, Shane?" she asked, finally getting the words out. "Because you know what happens when you order me around."

"You flip the tables. I know. But I'm asking you, Nicki." He held her hand to his chest, where his heart beat so loudly that it became her own. "Will you be there every night with me? For the rest of our lives?"

She nodded, dropping the champagne glass, hugging him until she didn't know where he ended and where she began.

She'd been waiting a long, long time for this—to be made absolutely complete by Shane Carter.

To take part in the ultimate role with the man she'd loved and would love forever.

* * * * *

PASSION

For a spicier, decidedly hotter read—
these are your destination for romances!

COMING NEXT MONTH
AVAILABLE NOVEMBER 22, 2011

#651 MERRY CHRISTMAS, BABY
Vicki Lewis Thompson,
Jennifer LaBrecque,
Rhonda Nelson

#652 RED-HOT SANTA
Uniformly Hot!
Tori Carrington

#653 THE MIGHTY QUINNS: KELLAN
The Mighty Quinns
Kate Hoffmann

#654 IT HAPPENED ONE CHRISTMAS
The Wrong Bed
Leslie Kelly

#655 SEXY SILENT NIGHTS
Forbidden Fantasies
Cara Summers

#656 SEX, LIES, AND MISTLETOE
Undercover Operatives
Tawny Weber

REQUEST YOUR FREE BOOKS!
2 FREE NOVELS PLUS 2 FREE GIFTS!

red-hot reads!

YES! Please send me 2 FREE Harlequin® Blaze™ novels and my 2 FREE gifts (gifts are worth about $10). After receiving them, if I don't wish to receive any more books, I can return the shipping statement marked "cancel." If I don't cancel, I will receive 6 brand-new novels every month and be billed just $4.49 per book in the U.S. or $4.96 per book in Canada. That's a saving of at least 14% off the cover price. It's quite a bargain. Shipping and handling is just 50¢ per book in the U.S. and 75¢ per book in Canada.* I understand that accepting the 2 free books and gifts places me under no obligation to buy anything. I can always return a shipment and cancel at any time. Even if I never buy another book, the two free books and gifts are mine to keep forever.

151/351 HDN FEQE

Name _____
(PLEASE PRINT)

Address _____ Apt. #

City _____ State/Prov. _____ Zip/Postal Code

Signature (if under 18, a parent or guardian must sign) _____

Mail to the **Reader Service:**
IN U.S.A.: P.O. Box 1867, Buffalo, NY 14240-1867
IN CANADA: P.O. Box 609, Fort Erie, Ontario L2A 5X3

Not valid for current subscribers to Harlequin Blaze books.

Want to try two free books from another line?
Call 1-800-873-8635 or visit www.ReaderService.com.

* Terms and prices subject to change without notice. Prices do not include applicable taxes. Sales tax applicable in N.Y. Canadian residents will be charged applicable taxes. Offer not valid in Quebec. This offer is limited to one order per household. All orders subject to credit approval. Credit or debit balances in a customer's account(s) may be offset by any other outstanding balance owed by or to the customer. Please allow 4 to 6 weeks for delivery. Offer available while quantities last.

Your Privacy—The Reader Service is committed to protecting your privacy. Our Privacy Policy is available online at www.ReaderService.com or upon request from the Reader Service.

We make a portion of our mailing list available to reputable third parties that offer products we believe may interest you. If you prefer that we not exchange your name with third parties, or if you wish to clarify or modify your communication preferences, please visit us at www.ReaderService.com/consumerchoice or write to us at Reader Service Preference Service, P.O. Box 9062, Buffalo, NY 14269. Include your complete name and address.

HBIIB

Lucy Flemming and Ross Mitchell shared a magical,
sexy Christmas weekend together six years ago.
This Christmas, history may repeat itself when they find
themselves stranded in a major snowstorm...
and alone at last.

Read on for a sneak peek from
IT HAPPENED ONE CHRISTMAS
by Leslie Kelly.

Available December 2011, only from Harlequin® Blaze™.

EYEING THE GRAY, THICK SKY through the expansive wall of windows, Lucy began to pack up her photography gear. The Christmas party was winding down, only a dozen or so people remaining on this floor, which had been transformed from cubicles and meeting rooms to a holiday funland. She smiled at those nearest to her, then, seeing the glances at her silly elf hat, she reached up to tug it off her head.

Before she could do it, however, she heard a voice. A deep, male voice—smooth and sexy, and so not Santa's.

"I appreciate you filling in on such short notice. I've heard you do a terrific job."

Lucy didn't turn around, letting her brain process what she was hearing. Her whole body had stiffened, the hairs on the back of her neck standing up, her skin tightening into tiny goose bumps. Because that voice sounded so familiar. *Impossibly* familiar.

It can't be.

"It sounds like the kids had a great time."

Unable to stop herself, Lucy began to turn around, wondering if her ears—and all her other senses—were deceiving her. After all, six years was a long time, the mind could play tricks. What were the odds that she'd bump into *him,* here? And today of all days. December 23.

Six years exactly. Was that really possible?

One look—and the accompanying frantic thudding of her heart—and she knew her ears and brain were working just fine. Because it was *him.*

"Oh, my God," he whispered, shocked, frozen, staring as thoroughly as she was. "Lucy?"

She nodded slowly, not taking her eyes off him, wondering why the years had made him even more attractive than ever. It didn't seem fair. Not when she'd spent the past six years thinking he must have started losing that thick, golden-brown hair, or added a spare tire to that trim, muscular form.

No.

The man was gorgeous. Truly, without-a-doubt, mouthwateringly handsome, every bit as hot as he'd been the first time she'd laid eyes on him. She'd been twenty-two, he one year older.

They'd shared an amazing holiday season.

And had never seen one another again.

Until now.

Find out what happens in
IT HAPPENED ONE CHRISTMAS
by Leslie Kelly.
Available December 2011, only from Harlequin® Blaze™

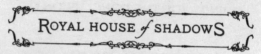

ROMANTIC
SUSPENSE

USA TODAY BESTSELLING AUTHOR

MARIE FERRARELLA

Brings you another exciting installment from

CAVANAUGH
JUSTICE

A Cavanaugh Christmas

When Detective Kaitlyn Two Feathers follows a kidnapping case outside her jurisdiction, she enlists the aid of Detective Thomas Cavelli. Still reeling from the discovery that his father was a Cavanaugh, Thomas takes the case, thinking it will be a nice distraction...until Kaitlyn becomes his ultimate distraction. As the case heats up and time is running out, Thomas must prove to Kaitlyn that he is trustworthy and risk it all for the one thing they both never thought they'd find—love.

Available November 22 wherever books are sold!

www.Harlequin.com

HRS27753

American ★ Romance®

LAURA MARIE ALTOM
brings you
another touching tale from

When family tragedy forces Wyatt Buckhorn to pair up
with his longtime secret crush, Natalie Poole, and care
for the Buckhorn clan's seven children, Wyatt worries
he's in over his head. Fearing his shameful secret will
be exposed, Wyatt tries to fight his growing attraction
to Natalie. As Natalie begins to open up to Wyatt,
he starts yearning for a family of his own—a family
with Natalie. But can Wyatt trust his heart enough
to reveal his secret?

A Baby in His Stocking

Available December
wherever books are sold!